A
GAME
IN
YELLOW

ALSO BY HAILEY PIPER

NOVELS

Queen of Teeth

No Gods for Drowning

Cruel Angels Past Sundown

A Light Most Hateful

All the Hearts You Eat

THE WORM AND HIS KINGS SERIES

The Worm and His Kings

Even the Worm Will Turn

Song of the Tyrant Worm

COLLECTIONS

Unfortunate Elements of My Anatomy

The Ghostlands of Natalie Glasgow

NOVELLAS

Cranberry Cove

Your Mind Is a Terrible Thing

Benny Rose the Cannibal King

The Possession of Natalie Glasgow

A
GAME
IN
YELLOW

Hailey Piper

SAGA PRESS

LONDON   NEW YORK   TORONTO
AMSTERDAM/ANTWERP   NEW DELHI   SYDNEY/MELBOURNE

1230 AVENUE OF THE AMERICAS, NEW YORK, NEW YORK 10020

For more than 100 years, Simon & Schuster has championed authors and the stories they create. By respecting the copyright of an author's intellectual property, you enable Simon & Schuster and the author to continue publishing exceptional books for years to come. We thank you for supporting the author's copyright by purchasing an authorized edition of this book.

No amount of this book may be reproduced or stored in any format, nor may it be uploaded to any website, database, language-learning model, or other repository, retrieval, or artificial intelligence system without express permission. All rights reserved. Inquiries may be directed to Simon & Schuster, 1230 Avenue of the Americas, New York, NY 10020 or permissions@simonandschuster.com.

This book is a work of fiction. Any references to historical events, real people, or real places are used fictitiously. Other names, characters, places, and events are products of the author's imagination, and any resemblance to actual events or places or persons, living or dead, is entirely coincidental.

Copyright © 2025 by Hailey Piper

All rights reserved, including the right to reproduce this book or portions thereof in any form whatsoever. For information, address Saga Press Subsidiary Rights Department, 1230 Avenue of the Americas, New York, NY 10020.

First Saga Press trade paperback edition August 2025

SAGA PRESS and colophon are trademarks of Simon & Schuster, LLC

Simon & Schuster strongly believes in freedom of expression and stands against censorship in all its forms. For more information, visit BooksBelong.com.

For information about special discounts for bulk purchases, please contact Simon & Schuster Special Sales at 1-866-506-1949 or business@simonandschuster.com.

The Simon & Schuster Speakers Bureau can bring authors to your live event. For more information or to book an event, contact the Simon & Schuster Speakers Bureau at 1-866-248-3049 or visit our website at www.simonspeakers.com.

Manufactured in the United States of America

1 3 5 7 9 10 8 6 4 2

Library of Congress Control Number: 2025935947

ISBN 978-1-6680-7708-5
ISBN 978-1-6680-7709-2 (ebook)

To the disasters like me

A GAME IN YELLOW

# 1

Breathe

THE CUT WAS QUIET, ALMOST silent. If Carmen had meant to stab something thin and soft, she would've held it up and run it through with steel, leaving nothing but air on the other side to absorb the point.

But she'd only stabbed anything at all because she was spacing out at her desk. The glow of her work monitor must've messed her up on some subliminal level, and she'd checked out of her brain hard enough to drive her seldom-used letter opener through her black mousepad. Only the steel clacking against the desk warned her anything had happened.

She nudged the mouse away and lifted the thin square of fabric and rubber, dangling it in front of her eyes. A small round hole let in the blue monitor light, as if the mousepad were a one-eyed mask.

Bad girl, she told herself.

She studied the letter opener—could a dull edge become a murder weapon? Of course. It was part of this dull office, a dozing animal with soulless white walls and piercing fluorescent lights, and that overwhelming dullness had to be a murder weapon, too, killing Carmen with a tedious blade. Or worse, smoothing out her personality and peeling away her features until it could render her a faceless peon.

She touched her cheek, thinking of tender fingers, and then checked the time. Five minutes to go. Almost end of day.

Foot tapping, blood teeming, thinking about what would happen later, a quickness in her heart—how was she supposed to concentrate with this kind of pressure and anticipation?

It's nerves, she thought. *Nothing worse.*

When she checked the time again, it was three minutes to six. She couldn't take the waiting anymore and began packing up her bag, logging out of her data-entry files, bounding out of her chair with a barked goodbye to her manager, Liza, before zipping away from the cubicles, out the door, and into the city.

September heat thickened the air across Queens. She was having enough trouble keeping her breath steady, but the walk to the nearest station to take the 7 was mercifully short. Her hands broke from her bag to hold her phone over the reader, and then she pressed through the turnstile toward the next westward train.

There, easily done. She was just one more person trying to get home.

And yet, a sense of separation haunted her through the ride. No one tried for the empty seats beside her at the few stops before her transfer. Not one person approached to ask for change at the Queensboro Plaza platform where she stood

A GAME IN YELLOW

waiting for her connecting train. As if every commuter and wanderer were smelling death on her.

They couldn't understand. There might be a sense of dying ahead, but on the other side, there was life.

A yellow N train screeched to a halt alongside the platform and poured out fresh commuters. Carmen squeezed aboard and stood by the door, looking out its west-facing windows.

The rail line toward Ditmars ran above the streets, sweeping past graffitied brick and flat rooftops. Beyond those, the windows offered a glimpse across the East River to the Manhattan skyline, its buildings rising in a jagged series of peaks as if the sky were grinning with a concrete underbite. Carmen thought of it scooping up the rest of the city. Bad omens lay everywhere.

She clutched her bag tight to her chest and tried to take slow breaths. There were only a few stops between Queensboro and her own, but each one felt like pumping the brakes on her heart, squeezing out another dose of adrenaline.

Her hands trembled by the time the train reached the 30th Avenue station. She hurried onto the platform, down the steps, and headed east, crossing a handful of streets and north a couple blocks. The storefronts and home windows seemed to lean toward her, even when she reached her apartment building, the brown brick becoming its eyes, watching, waiting. Every inch of Queens was vibrating.

Or maybe that was her. Nervous, excited, worried, scared. It could all go right for a change. It could all be terrible.

Don't be terrible, she told herself, as if that were in her control. Sometimes it felt like it should be. Shouldn't she know enough not to fuck up her life?

But control wasn't a concept she'd ever grasped. If she could take charge in a practical way, she would have done so already.

She yanked open the heavy door and hurried inside, past mailboxes, up the stairwell. The second floor looked darker today, but she barely caught any of it in her shaky rush toward her apartment. In pulling out her keys. Unlocking and opening the door. Letting it shut.

None of these features or sensations were as real as the feeling of a firm cylinder jamming against the back of her head. Her bag dropped to one side. She swallowed hard, mouth gone dry, and raised her hands, could practically imagine the pistol digging into her skull.

"Not smart, coming back here after what you pulled," a voice rich as caramel said, her tone lethal. "Not smart at all."

Minutes passed, too slow and yet too fast. Carmen was nude now, her button-up and slacks and everything else lying on the floor several feet away. Sweat made her bare skin stick where it touched this wooden chair. Her heart beat a gallop through her chest, but when she tried raising a hand to feel it through her sternum, her right wrist snagged on a leather cuff binding it to one arm of the chair. Another held her left wrist in place, and similar cuffs bound her ankles to the chair's legs.

A heat billowed behind her—Blanca, her hand stroking Carmen's short hair. Blanca, who'd restrained her.

Blanca, ready to end this.

"I can tell you things," Carmen said, mouth still dry. "Secrets."

A GAME IN YELLOW

"It's too late for that," Blanca said, almost doting. "Much too late."

Hazel eyes reflected in Carmen's vision for a blink, drifting dark circles like twin eclipses, before cloudy plastic wrenched against her face. It flattened across her brow, pressed down the tip of her pointy nose, and squeezed her strong chin, smothering all reflections in a whitish fog of exhalation.

Blanca tucked one arm over the rim of the stiff two-gallon freezer bag, sealing it to Carmen's throat. Her other hand slid up Carmen's head and laid a gentle hand on top. She kissed the outer plastic, her lower lip's two studs pressing cold to Carmen's temple while Carmen sucked in a breath that wouldn't come.

"I thought we had something special," Blanca said. "But you've fucked me over for the last time."

Seconds passed. Maybe a breathless minute. Carmen couldn't say how much time slid by before she began to fight. Couldn't see a clock. Couldn't open her mouth with Blanca gripping the bag beneath her jaw.

Blanca leaned close and kissed the plastic again. "And now, you can die for me." Her voice dropped to a whisper. "Die slowly, my love."

Carmen thrashed to one side, her naked legs rising slightly, but the restraints held firm. Her thighs thumped up and down against the chair, neck catching with Blanca's grip, and an inner fist tensed between her thighs.

No escape. Trapped in delicious suffocation and its ecstatic thrill.

Blanca unstuck the bag from Carmen's neck, only long

enough for a breath, and then hugged it to her again. Another terrifying, wonderful jolt rocked her body, and the tremble of Blanca's restrained laughter quaked into the chair. Controlling herself, keeping in character, yet overjoyed with Carmen's excitement.

Expectant over it.

A nervous pressure seized inside Carmen's chest.

Something wasn't right. Sweat dotted her skin, and a dampness pooled within the dark hair between her thighs, as certain as the condensation within the plastic bag, and a vivacious tingling lit her nerves down to her fingertips and toes.

These were neutral facts of no interest. Her body was ready to explode with asphyxiation-driven arousal, but her mind had eased to the stillness of an untouched pond, brightened with anticipation and shadowed by apathy and looming disappointment.

Why didn't she care? Blanca was doing everything right, even breathing against Carmen's ear to make her jealous for stolen air, but an indifferent darkness fogged her head. She should've been craving Blanca's touch by now. Lips, fingers, tongue, anything.

Ecstasy might come if she could hold out until death's precipice—

Carmen pincered her left thumb and middle fingertip, and then she snapped her fingers, the nonverbal safeword.

Blanca immediately unlatched from Carmen's head and throat, tearing the plastic away and giving space for Carmen to suck in the cool apartment air.

"That was fast," Blanca said. "You all right? Can you hear me?"

A GAME IN YELLOW

Carmen blinked hard, exhaled harder, and looked up, where the ceiling light cast a golden aura around a broad silhouette. The fog cleared at each blink until the silhouette became Blanca.

One dark eye sparkled; the other hid beneath draping coils of black hair. She was gorgeously fat and wore mocha-colored slacks and a same-colored suit jacket with no undershirt, exposing her bare fawn-brown sternum. The outfit suited her role of vengeful mobster in this scenario, icing out her snitching ex-lover, but something about her radiated the tragic beauty of a femme fatale. Maybe a switch-up would help. Carmen could be the mobster, murdered by the one woman she thought she could trust.

Except this beauty hadn't grown from their game. That was all Blanca. Carmen should have not only been awed by her presence but ravenous with desire.

Blanca creased her forehead in concern and cupped a tender palm to Carmen's cheek. "Pet?"

"I'm broken," Carmen said, breath steadying. "Disconnected. It isn't working."

Blanca slid a playful finger through Carmen's dark lower curls. "Feels like it's working."

"Not up here."

Carmen tried tapping her head, but the leather cuff again caught her wrist. Her brain hadn't come all the way back yet, and the surprise at forgetting she was bound almost brought momentary excitement.

Almost.

"I warned you this was a bad idea," Blanca said, unlatching

the wrist restraints. "Plastic is dangerous. You should've let me smother you with my belly or sit on your face."

Carmen was still catching her breath and couldn't explain how, much as she loved either suggestion, trying it would've broken the suspension of disbelief. No mobster would kill an ex-lover in that fashion.

Blanca lowered to one knee to free Carmen's ankles. "Maybe it's a bad idea all around. Safety first, remember? Tomorrow we could try—what was that one you liked?" She waved a hand in front of her face, snatching for the word she wanted. "The mask. It's been a minute since."

"No mask," Carmen said.

"Or the mermaid, caught by the sailor?" Blanca asked. "I could try a reverse Munter hitch down your legs."

Carmen nodded to spare Blanca's optimism, but tomorrow wouldn't improve anything. Same as the other nights they'd tried to heal whatever had gone wrong in Carmen's head.

That word again stroked the tip of her tongue—*broken*—and she couldn't shake it away as Blanca helped her stand up and draped a silky turquoise robe around her. It belonged to Blanca, but her belongings and scent brought relief, the way Blanca prioritized Carmen's aftercare even when they'd cut their rough scenario short.

She led them to the living room's lavender couch. "Cuddle and a movie?"

Another nod, and Carmen let herself be set down. Sometimes, like the moment Blanca returned to the couch with the TV remote, Carmen caught a look of coldness in her eyes. Far-away. Haunted. Uncertain if she was relieved, thinking breath-play was a bad idea, or disappointed, and why wouldn't she be?

A GAME IN YELLOW

She had put a lot of thought and work into this, ensuring safety so that Carmen could have her little death fantasy without worry. Blanca kept control; Blanca would make it okay. Love was a muscle, and she kept it toned. She wanted to see Carmen happy despite her own reservations.

All that, only for Carmen to pull the plug. As if the threat of asphyxiation couldn't offer a powerful enough high, staring down death's cliff. For Blanca to agree at all hinted how desperate she'd become to shatter this carapace around Carmen's enthusiasm and joy.

"Will you lie on me?" Carmen asked. It came out with the meekness of asking, *Do you still love me?*

Blanca flashed a faint smile. "For a little, before my shift."

And Carmen had to hope that was the answer to the spoken question and not the unspoken one.

Maybe she was causing her own trouble. She had been stewing in her juices through work, possibly over-anticipated. Her excitement might have bled dry across the day. Maybe they needed to be more spontaneous? Except Blanca wouldn't like that. It wasn't safe.

Carmen stretched across the couch, waiting. Blanca slid out of her suit, dressed herself in another robe, and reclined over Carmen's lithe frame, her comforting softness reshaping around Carmen like a weighted blanket made of girlfriend. The pressure slowed Carmen's breathing, not in the game's elusive sensuality, but a calm she absorbed from Blanca into her muscles and mind. Maybe seeing that despondent look in Blanca's eyes was Carmen's projection, nothing more.

Or maybe she echoed Carmen's worry, and they were feeding each other's anxieties in a forever loop like an orbiting meteor building momentum before one planet could slingshot it into another.

Carmen couldn't face that extinction event. She needed to figure out what was wrong with her enthusiasm and remind it how much she wanted Blanca, wholly and utterly and in every possible way like she deserved, and soon.

Before their conjoined anxiety dragged them out of their game, their world, and tore their hearts to shreds.

2

The Possibilities

RUNNING LATE TO WORK AGAIN, Carmen's usual. No real excuse, only slow to start and far too trusting of rail-line schedules.

Swinging by Dan's Bagel Deli and picking up an assortment for the office would smooth over her tardiness, along with an egg sandwich to appease her manager. She texted while slipping through the deli's front door.

CARMEN: In line at deli, be in soon.

Liza answered with a thumbs-up and an egg. In twenty minutes, Carmen would stumble into the office, the bangs of her short chestnut hair clinging to her sweaty forehead, her button-up disheveled, breath chugging as if Blanca had only now let her out from beneath a plastic hood. Everyone would think Carmen had come running, forgiven thanks to the bagel box clutched in her arms. Problem solved. Given a moment, she could fix any situation.

Except your sex life. She gritted her teeth and wished the suggestion away, but she had no safeword against intrusive thoughts.

Eighteen minutes later, she arrived at the office disheveled and sweaty, as predicted. Her coworkers greeted her with waves and hellos from where they clustered around one girl's cubicle before Carmen steered herself into the nearby breakroom to unpack the bagels, plastic knives, and schmear alongside Liza's foil-wrapped egg sandwich.

So much effort to keep a pointless, impersonal job. Anyone could cross that Brillo pad of a carpet, sit at those computers, and peck at a distressingly quiet keyboard. LeviTek, or Info-Seam, or whatever was the company's name after half a dozen owner changes, hired the fastest fingers. For what? Data entry meant condensing people's entire lives to fillable boxes on a computer monitor, and the bloodlines of commerce passed the information from one office to another, forming a great greedy organism of insurance bullshit, advertising parasitism, and statistical horrors meant to help digest the world.

And yet it presented itself with the abject mundanity of a breakroom and cubicle rows. Carmen had to remind herself she worked a mere eight hours a day here. She could have it worse.

Only when the last bit of cream cheese crossed her tongue did she realize she'd devoured an entire bagel without noticing. Resentment toward work had distracted her. What was she trying to avoid thinking about again?

Oh, right—Blanca. The endless fuck-ups with beautiful Blanca.

A GAME IN YELLOW

Carmen started putting together another sorrow-smothering bagel, one she'd taste this time, as the other office women encircled the breakroom table to titter and feign reluctance.

"Thank you, Carmen."

"Happy Friday!"

"Cheesy junk goes straight to my hips. Who wants to split one?"

"Me. I look fat enough in this skirt already, and I want to look nice for the anniversary party."

"On your second already, Carmen? I wish I could eat like you."

Yes, they did wish they could eat like Carmen. Another bagel. A taste from between Blanca's thighs. Except none of them would appreciate her, terrified of seeing anyone like Blanca, of looking like Blanca. *Hips, fat, eat,* they complained. Like those were bad things, jabbing needly tongues into Blanca's sides.

Not exactly like you're pleasing her, Carmen reminded herself.

She watched the other women pluck vulturelike at the spread, unsure the bagel carcasses were dead yet, and then carried her tote bag, her second bagel, and Liza's egg sandwich to her cubicle. She kept few belongings there. A calendar showing cheerful art from *My Neighbor Totoro* hung by a tack from the wall, a gift from Blanca, and a trilobite fossil, gifted by an ex, was Carmen's makeshift paperweight.

Most important was the small framed photo of Blanca. Whenever work became a soul-sucking vacuum, Carmen only had to glance over. Think of Blanca. Flash back to any moment of holding her, of being held, since they'd met that night Carmen stopped in the pub where Blanca used to bartend two years ago, and then that weekend shortly after when they moved in together and grabbed hold of each other and didn't let go.

Until the disconnect in Carmen. No idea where it had come from or when it would heal.

Clever Blanca—she'd found detours. They already enjoyed light bondage and roleplay. Wrists bound here, a blindfold there, spread across the bed. Time they spent developing the spoken safeword—*dimetrodon*—and the unspoken snapping of fingers for when speech became impossible. Shibari joined Blanca's skill set as Carmen's disconnect worsened, with Blanca's deft hands turning Carmen's slight figure almost decorative. They tried latex, and when that ceased to work, they moved to pain in its many flavors. Wax, whips, and worse.

Role-oriented deathlike breathplay was last week's experiment, but Carmen's investment remained elusive. She was sputtering, and Blanca was running out of ideas.

A fist knocked on Carmen's cubicle wall, and she jerked in her rolling chair to find Liza Medina staring down at her. She was in her mid-fifties, tall as gods, dark hair dyed blond except at the roots. One T-shirted arm slung over the cubicle wall, an olive hand reaching out with an expectant upturned palm.

"That a new paperweight?" Liza said. "Or do I spy a sandwich of mine?"

Carmen apologized and handed over the foiled bundle. "Rushed too fast," she said. "Lightheaded."

"You don't eat enough, string bean." Liza chucked the sandwich up and down, and it gave a crunch at each landing. "Don't listen to these starvation fetishists. They're so airheaded, you could use them to clean out the copier. Not that that'll fix it." She winked and headed back to her office.

A GAME IN YELLOW

Carmen couldn't help a smirk. *Fetishists.* If only Liza knew.

But there was an idea—starvation, but of the sexual kind. Carmen could borrow a page from the evangelicals who'd stalked her adolescence, starving herself of sex until desire forced the concept itself to undergo resurrection. Blanca could order Carmen a chastity belt.

Or would abstinence kill her sex drive entirely? If so, how long until that killed the relationship? Was sex even the true problem?

Maybe Carmen didn't like herself anymore. Everything felt like a chore. Her commute. Work itself. Even eating, sometimes. A memo sat in her email, reminding her there was a mandatory synergistic workshop in the Catskills in late September, a couple weeks after the company's acquisition anniversary party, paid for by the office's latest owner.

And while her coworkers chirped about how fun and beautiful it might be to get away for a couple days, all Carmen could think of were excuses not to go.

Wherever she went, she was stuck with herself.

She studied her face in the bathroom mirror at midday, assessing her sharp jawline, pinkish complexion, yellow-green stare, short stature—she might not fuck herself were she doubled, but nothing made her wish to escape her skin.

The signal break was not between body and Blanca, only between body and mind.

And yet it had everything to do with Blanca. If she broke things off, Carmen would break shortly after.

Maybe she had depression. She considered talking to a therapist as she traveled back to her cubicle. Thought some more on it while rattling out the names, heights, weights, phone numbers, and addresses of strangers into her computer. She would have to find an affordable counselor in her insurance network. And the right one who would understand that women liked sex. And one who wouldn't have an issue with that sex being same-sex.

By day's end, all the consideration left her exhausted and hollow. She didn't know what dragged at her insides and made the flames of passion sputter like a campfire facing a hurricane.

She only knew thirty-five was too young to feel this dull.

~

Carmen found Blanca humming to herself when she opened the apartment door. She stood at the sink of their small corner kitchen, hips rocking to her own tune, the faucet splashing water over a glass and masking the sounds of locks and hinges.

The apartment wasn't large, but they'd made it their own. A white-covered novel sat face down on their tiny kitchen table, alongside a stack of other books and an empty flowerpot. Four chairs surrounded the table. Towels were draped over one of them to hide the wear and tear of bindings and sweat. Beyond the kitchen, the TV sat on a desk against the living room wall, facing the couch and a weathered recliner. A window looked out on the city, surrounded by dark-violet walls. They'd hung up a few photos of themselves near the bathroom, but mostly they'd gathered art from the street and dressed the living room in warm paintings and twisted tin sculptures of small birds, lizards, and butterflies, as if the walls themselves bubbled with life.

Their bedroom door hung open on peaceful light-blue walls and a hill of pillows bound in a ceiling net. Beside it, another doorway opened to the spare bedroom. Most tenants might have rented it out.

A GAME IN YELLOW

Carmen and Blanca had instead converted it into their sexual playroom. They'd purchased most of the stuff inside before the last two rent hikes. Blanca would've likely sold some of it to ease future financial strain if there were any profitable market for hand-me-down sex toys.

Only recently had they moved the game to the living room. Blanca hoped a change of scenery might mend whatever was wrong with Carmen.

Not that Blanca ever put it that way. Her girlfriend was perfect in her eyes.

But Carmen knew better.

She watched Blanca peel off yellow dish gloves and studied the dark hair cascading down the back of her blouse. A hunch in her shoulders said she was hurting this afternoon. Thirty-three seemed too young for aching, but she stood proud. The women at Carmen's office could only imitate this pride, and likely Blanca wouldn't have noticed their disdainful remarks. Advertisements, rude comments—none of it mattered. She possessed a mastery of self few people dreamed of, and she wouldn't care whether Carmen's coworkers meant to offend or please her.

Anger had been a convenient and powerful distraction, enough for Carmen to briefly bury her problems. Small wonder many men loved the feeling.

But anger couldn't solve this. Carmen shut the apartment door at last, and Blanca's ears perked up.

"Hey," Carmen said. "That's my job."

She'd taken up cleaning responsibilities shortly after they moved in together. Sometimes as part of the game, more because Blanca's part-timing at the café and part-timing at the bar meant she had enough mess to handle already.

She didn't say anything at first. The yellow gloves hit the sink basin as she turned around and bounced from kitchen tile to carpet. A luminance climbed Carmen's insides, and her eyes shimmered with almost-tears as Blanca crashed into her with a fierce hug.

You'll lose her. She'll think you don't love her anymore, and then you'll lose her, and you'll deserve it.

Carmen swallowed the vicious thought. "Missed you, too," she said.

"I've been waiting all day to tell you," Blanca said, giddy in Carmen's ear. "I found something that might help you."

Carmen smiled into Blanca's hair. "Really?"

"Really. I met someone."

"Oh." Carmen pursed her lips.

They had brought temporary partners into the game before, but half the time they seemed more hassle than fun. She didn't want to play the killjoy today. Not with that spring in Blanca's step, and not when she'd been waiting for Carmen's homecoming to share the news.

"Cool," Carmen said, desperate to sound elated. "Are they joining the game tonight? Tomorrow?"

Blanca broke from the hug, and the sweet earthen darkness of her eyes beamed good cheer into Carmen's face. "No, we're going out. We go to her. Tonight." Her gaze flicked up and down, scrutinizing the tiniest fault lines in Carmen's expression. "This is something different, I promise. That's what we need, right? Something different?"

She said *we*, but she wasn't the problem. Her sex drive could start as easily as sliding a key into a new car's ignition, complete control of self. What she meant was *you*. What *you* need.

A GAME IN YELLOW

"Something different," Carmen echoed.

It came out more hopeful than she felt. That climbing light inside her must have finally found her tongue and laced it with trust and adoration toward Blanca, who scrunched her nose with another smile and then bounced away.

Giving up would break her heart. And breaking her heart would mean Carmen had blown the best thing that ever happened to her. For Blanca, she could wear the mask of optimism. She could even play the part if they brought hopefulness into the game. Blanca was worth it.

Carmen turned to the living room, and she made damn well sure to smile. "How should I dress?"

3

The Smoking Section

MANHATTAN'S BALMY SEPTEMBER AIR CLUNG to Carmen's skin as she and Blanca left the downtown subway platform. The red sunset cast lengthening shadows from the apartment buildings, patterning the streets, alleyways, and doorsteps in still-humid shade.

"We're almost there," Blanca said, though she remained cagey about where *there* might be.

"It isn't Raspberry Swirl, is it?" Carmen asked, scowling.

"That's still in Queens."

"I know, but you could be taking me on a detour. Throwing me off."

"No," Blanca said. "Not a detour, not the Swirl."

Carmen should have known better. Blanca's dress code instruction had been *nice, but comfortable*, and that wouldn't suit a classy fetish club like Raspberry Swirl, no matter how much Blanca used to frequent the place. She wore a white lily-patterned blouse and matching skirt. Carmen wore a green-gray tank top and pinstripe slacks.

"A professional dom, then?" Carmen asked.

"We can't afford that right now," Blanca said. "Rent's going up in January."

"Again? Hell." Carmen wondered how much, but Blanca controlled the finances. She had the better head for it, among other things. "Is it psychedelics?"

"We can't afford that either. Weed is enough." Blanca gave Carmen's hip a love tap. "Your body belongs to me, and my body's a temple. The kind that runs on blood, not shrooms."

The word *temple* sent Carmen's thoughts racing in another direction. "Is it a shaman? Some kind of magic, like a bruja?"

"If magic were real, I wouldn't mess with it. But this isn't magic." Blanca walked in silence for a moment, lips rubbing together as she hunted and pounced on the right words. "It's just weird shit. Completely different from anything you're thinking."

Her lack of clarity only made Carmen's skin tingle, either from humidity or the thrill of surprise. Either way, Carmen was ready; she—

Expected disappointment. Her excitement sweated out, assuming a lackluster night was inevitable, which only sent her anticipation plummeting toward pessimism. It was that feedback loop again. Stress begetting stress. She doubted Blanca could fix it, wherever they were going.

Wherever they had arrived. Blanca stopped on the sidewalk to pluck a compact mirror from her purse and fiddle with her lip studs, and then her gaze fixed ahead, where concrete steps climbed to the front door of a brown-brick apartment building. Sun-weathered wooden planks crossed its first-floor windows. The second- and third-floor windows gaped open like jagged glass teeth.

Carmen shuddered in the unseasonal heat. "Who lives here?"

"No one. Like nobody lives in a bunch of places anymore. They just"—Blanca gestured down the block—"sit there. But people gather anyway."

Blanca climbed the short steps and yanked the front door open, a slouching wooden slab with little motivation for clinging to its hinges. A grim stairwell opened to the left. Blanca led Carmen past it, onto a patchy purple hallway carpet, visible only by the narrow path breaking through the piled garbage bags and detritus like an animal trail over grass in the small rural town where Carmen grew up.

She pushed the reminder away. Hometown thoughts would kill any desire before Blanca had a chance to try her weird solution.

Former apartments hung open, their walls patchy with dark holes. Music blasted from dim corridors, where indiscernible figures were rubbing powder across tables and grinding against each other.

"Drugs, but not for us?" Carmen asked. "Is this an exhibitionist thing?"

"So many questions," Blanca said. "Quiet down and trust me, all right?"

A red EXIT sign glared at the hall's end. Carmen guessed the back door opened onto an alley and iron fire escape, but before she could touch the handle, Blanca steered them into a sullen gray room. A twenty-something man in a deep red hoodie sat in a fold-out chair beside a dark opening in the floor.

He glanced up at Blanca's footsteps. "Who goes? What's your business?"

"Blanca Balmaceda-Lugo. Carmen Mancini. Heading to Underside."

The man waved a gloved hand, signaling for Blanca and Carmen to descend clanging metal stairs that ended at a concrete floor. A wide room opened around them. Sleeping bags lined its walls, and the sounds of giggling, moaning, and puking echoed off the hard surfaces. Two skeletal women sat atop derelict washing machines, tossing tarot cards between them.

"Do they know you?" Carmen whispered.

"They just want a name and a reason," Blanca whispered back. "Especially if they need to kick you out."

"Looks like anything goes."

Blanca tittered. "I should've brought a gag for you."

In the broad basement's corner, another hole opened, where rickety planks led to a dingy subbasement. Carmen had heard of the old subway having rest areas for workers, now closed off from modern tunnels and yet accessible from secret places throughout the city. Some had been converted into subterranean speakeasies during Prohibition. Others lay forgotten. Or secret.

"How far down?" Carmen asked.

"Pet. Quiet." Blanca tossed her hair over one shoulder and softened her tone. "This is the last."

Another man waited in a forking hallway below, old and

colossal and yet pale like he never went upstairs to see the sun. He asked no questions, only waved a narrow flashlight. His breathing came loud in the dim.

"Smoking section," Blanca said.

The under-street man aimed his flashlight to Blanca's left. She followed the beam, and Carmen followed her down a thin hallway where a golden glow pulsed from behind a beaded curtain.

"What did you say?" Carmen asked. "Are we going to smoke?" She realized a moment too late that she'd broken Blanca's command.

Blanca didn't seem to notice. "It's the area with the one we're seeing. Her name is Smoke."

She parted the beaded curtain onto dusky light. Rumbling conversation climbed from nearby tables alongside curls of smoke, clouding the golden bulbs above. Cheap bangles danced from ceiling-bound wires whenever anyone brushed past them. Scarlet-and-gold tapestries decorated the walls with pretty patterns, and a faraway neon sign glowed the words UNDERSIDE: SMOKING SECTION. Bodies jostled along a bar at the back, next to which a faded pink-and-green jukebox torn out of the 1960s played a guitar riff probably older than Carmen's parents.

Blanca interrupted Carmen's awestruck observation with a shout in her ear. "I got directions! Back corner!"

They slid between packed tables, the crowd a twitching organism mimicking a subway platform during rush hour. Some patrons tried to dance, but there was little room. Wires chased from the jukebox, the bar, and the neon sign into the ceiling. They were likely siphoning power from the city's main line.

The underground bustle thinned at the back corner, where a crescent-shaped booth formed a circle of cracked leather seating around a sleek wooden table.

Facing the room sat a striking woman in her late thirties, her features a mix of pale wolfen eyes, an elfin smirk, and hawkish talons jutting from three of five digits on her right hand. Finger tattoos brandished the playing card symbols of diamond, club, heart, and spade on her left. Lengthy russet curls snaked around her marble-white cheeks and over her black sequined top. Vermillion trousers covered her knees, pressing together against the table's edge.

She stuffed her phone in a forest-green satchel when she spotted Blanca. "Hey there, B." She had a melodious voice fit for a singer. "And Carmen, I presume."

Carmen mouthed, *Smoke?*

Blanca gave a curt nod and squeezed into the circular booth, dragging Carmen down beside her. "We met last night at the bar and got talking."

Smoke's gaze wandered from Carmen to Blanca and back. "Blanca tells me you need stimulation of a kind."

Carmen hid a frown behind her hand. *Got talking? Stimulation?* Blanca never chatted about their sex life outside her friend group. Which meant she was getting desperate, and Carmen had done that to her, and now she wanted to sink beneath the table and hide.

"It's like I told you," Blanca said.

"Right. About your game." Smoke plucked a pastel-pink vape pen from a ceramic coaster, inhaled sharply, and let white mist snake between her teeth. "But is your game ripe for the arcane?"

A GAME IN YELLOW

Carmen raised her eyebrows at Blanca. "You said it wasn't magic."

"Not magic," Smoke said. "Calling it magic is like calling psychiatry witchcraft. It's unenlightened. Come on, girl, this isn't the sticks. The jewels of the world and the pearls of all wisdom converge into the globality of mankind. And beyond."

She opened the mouth of her satchel and drew out a thin leathery book. Ragged white string bound its covers. Tan coloring clawed at its spine. Its front was pale and lumpy as if someone had scalded its face with bleach, and yet black stitched-on lettering spoke the title from beneath the scars.

The King in Yellow.

Carmen leaned over the table for a better look. The book seemed nothing special, but there was a gravity in its unspecialness. Too mundane an outer shell to be truly dull like her.

"This isn't addictive, is it?" Blanca asked.

"Only psychologically." Smoke set her vape pen atop the coaster and began to untie the book's string. "Ever stood at a cliff's edge? Or a skyscraper's? The height reaches up your legs, vertigo at the edge of life and death. That's one wild trip. And your heart racing when you pull back? That's life. True living."

An acrophobic tingling lit Carmen's skin. She forced away thoughts of childhood hiking and stuck to thoughts of rooftop ledges.

Smoke finished untying the string and cracked open the leather binding. Loose yellow pages, unglued from the book's gutter, wafted in the tailwind of its front cover. Their tattered edges surrounded typewritten ink, faded in some places, thick in others, their typist desperate to run an ink ribbon to its last drop before reloading their typewriter.

Carmen's eyes blurred as she glanced over the book. "A story?"

Smoke sucked at her vape again. "A play."

She was right—the first page showed not a title or chapter page, but a description and dialogue, with the text at the top reading *Act II*.

A wry laugh bubbled up Carmen's throat as she turned to Blanca. "You brought us here to read?"

"Try," Blanca said, chinning at the tome.

Harsh nails pinched Carmen's chin and guided her gaze back across the table. "It's no common book," Smoke said. "Ordinarily, you read the words. But these pages? They read you, too."

Carmen jerked her head from Smoke's grasp. "Okay?"

Smoke tucked her cheek into one hand and blew white mist over the book. "It's said that all who read *The King in Yellow* lose their minds. Or what looks like losing their minds. I've seen it happen. But if you try it and get away, the survivor's euphoria is magnificent."

Carmen eyed the yellowy pages again. She had agreed with Blanca that they needed something different, but this was bizarre.

Wasn't that the point, though? What could be more different than weird shit? And besides, Carmen's body worked fine. It was her mind that couldn't get with the sexual program. And same with any reading, your mind did the work, using the book's information to mold thoughts into fresh concepts.

Carmen glanced at Blanca, her dark eyes expectant, her smile earnest. If Blanca believed this had a chance of working, shouldn't Carmen be willing to give it a try? For her?

A GAME IN YELLOW

Smoke drummed her nails on the table. "Think of it like playing chicken. Two cars rushing at each other, but no one wants to die. Who swerves first? Reading these pages is the same. Read only enough to inhale the danger without living the catastrophe, and somewhere between terror and madness lies ecstasy."

Static reached through Carmen's fingers and toes. She could dismiss it as the excitement of an overactive imagination, conjuring rooftop ledge vertigo.

But since when had her imagination been this active?

A gentle hand took Carmen's—Blanca, soft and sweet and smiling. Carmen squeezed Blanca's hand in return. She had no faith in this, but she could try it out for the sake of finding a path forward.

"Okay," Carmen said, taking a deep breath. *For Blanca, for Blanca.* It was a chant. And a promise.

Carmen slid her hand from Blanca's grasp, gave Smoke a doubtful glance, and then focused on the first crisp yellow page:

Act II—Scene 1.

Upon the shores of Hali, the great steps climb forever and endless toward the amber skies above the city of Hastur, above the city of Alar, above the beauty of lost Carcosa, a redundant title, for all places beneath the twin black suns of the Hyades are lost.

4

Good Pet

A HEAVY CLAP SHOT CARMEN to sitting straight and gasping. The air slid over her tongue, soupy and thick with a smoky taste. She couldn't cough, could only manage shallow panting. Had she been holding her breath the entire time she'd been reading? For how long? She couldn't remember what she'd been reading, only this sudden shock through her system.

Smoke's splayed hand rested atop the shut leather cover. "That's enough for now."

Blanca petted Carmen's arm. "You all right?"

The question was too vague. Carmen didn't know how to answer, hands trembling, skin dotted with sweat. Her heart throbbed, a vicious caged animal, while a violent thrill stiffened her insides as if all her blood had gone ramrod straight. This had to be what a cock felt like if it could grow to five feet, four inches.

That thought was alien. Had she read it in Smoke's play? She couldn't remember. The words had slid from page to eyes to mind more as a feeling than a performance. She couldn't guess how many pages she'd read or why her body quaked beside Blanca. Was it terror? Or yearning? The difference muddled in some inner primordial ooze, Carmen's brain reduced from human complexity to ancestor reptiles of pre-dinosauric times, hunted by giant spiders, narrowly escaping tremendous hairy mandibles, and now she needed to indulge the lizard part of her brain's simple truth.

Book closed. Back from the ledge. Escaped the predator.

Panting hard, she turned to Blanca, whose face was a bright brown haze clouded by some ethereal aphrodisiac. It was time to scream. Or to lash out. To grab hold of Blanca in her softest places and not let go.

Blanca's pupils became twin eclipses against the whites of her eyes. Did she see the terror-yearning or yearn-terror in Carmen's expression, the *need*? She had to. Clever Blanca, beautiful Blanca, necessary Blanca.

"Somewhere private?" Blanca asked in a rush.

Smoke aimed one black-taloned finger. "Ladies' room."

Blanca shimmied out of the booth's circle and tugged Carmen through Underside's smoky haze. Carmen's muscles tensed down her back and sent a throbbing into her deepest places all the way to the ladies' room.

They scarcely made it to the sinks. Blanca parked herself atop the marble counter, and Carmen climbed onto her lap and tore into her.

Hot breath in Blanca's hair. Teeth at her neck. Slacks loosing from Carmen's hips and collapsing to the floor. Carmen latching her thighs around Blanca's leg in an awkward grind over Blanca's knee. A hand at Blanca's breast. Another grasping her side. Lips to lips. To shoulder. To burning, and breathing, and dripping.

A lake within me, Lake of Hali.

Nonsense in Carmen's thoughts. Her head was gone, and she didn't care. There was no Underside, no surface, only her grasping at Blanca's curves and kisses until wild animal shrieking banged through the restroom, a world collapsing in the back of Carmen's throat.

She slowed then, nipping at Blanca's arm, her belly, her hand as she petted Carmen's cheek.

"Better?" Blanca asked.

Carmen didn't answer. She took to her again, sliding her leg between Blanca's thighs, kissing the tender place at Blanca's collar that for reasons unknown shot lightning bolts through Blanca's skin, a storm rising until Blanca answered Carmen's teeth with a bite into Carmen's shoulder. Her muffled scream quaked through Carmen's muscles, where she could absorb and make them part of her.

They slowed. Caught their breath. Kissed again. Carmen collapsed against the wall, apathetic to every filthy surface, and then dressed herself.

Blanca led them from Underside, up concrete steps, metal ones, crossing blocks and subways to reach home, where they clutched each other in the shower, Carmen's heart again bursting with yearn-terror-lust-love.

They eventually collapsed as tangled midnight creatures, damp atop their bedsheets. Carmen melted into a pool of self, forgetting her skeletal structure, her thoughts, reduced to a wad of bubble gum some rude cosmic chewer had stuck to the surface of the world.

"We didn't say goodbye to Smoke," she muttered.

That sent them both giggling. Carmen kissed across Blanca's body and then curled into her, small against Blanca's chest.

A worrying darkness wormed into Carmen. She'd become so used to diminishing returns and mental apathy, she hadn't considered finding a solution. And now that she had, there was the chance to lose it. Because the solution didn't belong to her.

"It'll happen again, right?" Carmen asked, nuzzling Blanca's chin. "It won't be the last time?"

Blanca hummed against Carmen's ear. "It won't be the last time, Pet. I promise. We'll see Smoke again."

5

The Golden Masquerade

Within the palace of Hastur, overlooking the Lake of Hali, a grand ballroom shines with golden chandeliers and crystalline furnishing, a lure and respite for the city nobles. They enter left and right and down the ornate staircase in resplendent suits and lavish ballgowns. Each wears a fantastical mask or holds one in front of their face. Their garments come in many colors, but the masks are shades of ivory and gold, cream and amber, white and yellow, shaped as wolves and birds and impossible mollusks. It is the time of the golden masquerade.

Enter CARMEN. She wears a canary-yellow ballgown with sparkling trim; great dusky feathers tuft from its shoulders and back as if plucked from a living phoenix. She looks left and right, bewildered. Her mask is divine, a sleek disguise protruding like a beak or a snout, but too slight for her to tell its exact shape without taking it off. She only knows it is colored with glorious gold.

CARMEN   Has anyone seen my intended?

No one answers. The sounds of bustle and conversation stir around her, joining the sweet music of a harpist.

CARMEN   Isn't this exactly like me? Come to a masquerade without coordinating disguises. What's the significance in this?

Enter CAMILLA. She crosses the dancing nobles and professional conversationalists, her ballgown white as teeth, her feline mask hazy with the golden shade that circles the twin black suns in the sky.

CAMILLA   The significance, you ask? In a game of masks?

CARMEN   And you are?

CAMILLA takes CARMEN by the arm.

CAMILLA   Perhaps I am Camilla. Perhaps not. Anonymity thrives in the golden masquerade. Any mask might hide any face. We could find sweet Calliope, and recognize Carissa's heavenly gait, and naturally her sister Cassia is here, and we know the

A GAME IN YELLOW

                    graceful voice of Cassilda. An evening of possibilities. Even King Hastur might walk among his people in disguise. Who's to say?

CARMEN   None of us.

CAMILLA   None until the Hour of Unmasking, at sunset. For now, we must all be as strangers. Therefore, I might be Camilla. Or Camilla might be there, or there. You might be Camilla. You might be anyone.

CARMEN   Sunset? I see the suns sinking already.

CAMILLA   Slowly, my love. In time, they will slip beneath the horizon, their reflections no longer glowering upon the surface of Hali. Then, the unmasking. And then you may have yourself back, if you want her.

CAMILLA pulls CARMEN close, her snouted mask near enough to kiss.

CAMILLA   Or you might find you enjoy your disguise, and then the Hour of Unmasking will strip everything from you. Those are the stakes of the game.

~

Carmen stumbled backward, arms flailing. "What the hell?"

Her heart was a fly writhing against a spiderweb, frantic like she'd read again from Smoke's leatherbound tome. Some play or another dripped from her mind, but she couldn't have been reading. Smoke held *The King in Yellow* somewhere else in the city. Carmen had only been sleeping. Dreaming.

And sleepwalking.

She stood on bare feet, as naked as she'd gone to bed, but she'd left Blanca and their bed and their blue bedroom. A screwdriver lay in her hand. She must've grabbed it from the kitchen utility drawer in her sleep, her mind preoccupied with golden dreams, and now she'd carried it here.

Orange light burned through the parted curtain of the street-facing window of the playroom, illuminating its cardinal walls. Various sex toys sat in plastic containers along one shelf. A cushiony bench stretched at the floor's center, its sides offering wide iron loops for taking on rope. Sapphic art prints adorned most walls, some erotic, some benignly nude, one showing a pomegranate split around two exploratory fingers, ripe with seeds and flesh.

A kinder-looking damage than Carmen had inflicted on one wall. She'd apparently plunged the screwdriver through the plaster. And one stabbing wasn't good enough for somnambulistic Carmen. Twin wounds formed circles in the red wall like black sockets on a skinned face.

Her hand twitched, an unhelpful impulse to drop the screwdriver, but it didn't belong here. Work tools went in the utility drawer. This room was for play.

Playing with myself, Carmen thought.

She glanced at the pomegranate art, and then back to the wall, imagining warm wet fingers closing around hers. Gloryholes, of a kind, as if someone stood beyond the plaster, waiting for Carmen to reach into the liminal insides. She could almost feel something's breath.

A GAME IN YELLOW

And then she heard it in the wall—no, past the wall, in the adjoining bedroom. Blanca was snoring.

Carmen laughed at herself. No sound in the world could lull her to sleep like Blanca's gentle purring. She was silly for being scared.

Enough. She grabbed a framed art print off another wall, depicting a woman lying on a beach at dawn, the tide having draped her with a curious mermaid, and then swapped the screwdriver for glue strips and stuck the art print over the stab wounds in the plaster.

She then went back to bed.

6

The Waning

WHAT REMAINED OF THE DREAM trickled away over the weekend. By the start of work on Monday morning, it was the slightly discolored patch of mental pavement after a puddle's evaporation—

Under twin suns.

—leaving behind only a pulsing need. It reminded Carmen of Friday night's frisky subterranean tumble with Blanca, whose photo made Carmen antsy in her rolling cubicle seat, crossing her legs, uncrossing, recrossing. Every movement brought fresh desire, skin crawling, bones craving, a nerve thrumming between her thighs. She would have masturbated in the office restroom, as Liza had confessed to doing once when drunk at the last Christmas party, were there any guarantee for silence.

She instead had to wait until she got home. On Blanca's free evenings, they squished together in a delightful mess of grasping, kissing, clutching, laughing. Other nights, Carmen satisfied herself.

There wasn't time for elaborate games, only simple intimacy. The energy was too frantic in Carmen's flesh, the need immediate, and Blanca seemed too happy to want otherwise, letting an evening off from work sprawl into a night of skin against skin, as if they were trying to fuse into a single sapphic creature.

It took days for Carmen's mind to rediscover the disconnect.

~

A week of virile enthusiasm was a gift in itself. No sense pouting over a comedown from that strange high, especially when Carmen had predicted it couldn't last.

But she didn't want Blanca to know. Hard to manage that— Blanca noticed everything. Carmen's moods. Small changes in the apartment. She couldn't have missed the mermaid art print's new location in the playroom, but she either hadn't peeked behind it or chose not to say anything to Carmen about the stab wounds in the plaster. A mercy. Blanca was good at those.

Carmen felt her insides becoming a lighter running low on fuel. Her thumb could keep hitting the spark wheel, and maybe she'd get lucky and summon a flame, but the effect was waning.

~

The game was her idea. A desperate thumb dragging at that spark wheel again and again, hoping to light an inferno in her heart. She'd even take a faint ember. Anything to keep Blanca from wondering.

Music poured from Blanca's phone, set on the coffee table,

A GAME IN YELLOW

some playlist Carmen always thought of as *stoner guitar*. Pink Floyd tracks, the Futurelics, something else Carmen couldn't identify, the music mellow, not really going anywhere.

Neither was Carmen.

"Keep still," Blanca said. "You're interrupting me."

Carmen hunched on her knees where they'd shoved the coffee table toward the TV, with the front of the couch facing her side. Firm knots held her wrists together in front of her, arms bound to her thighs and stuck between her legs, where another thin rope coiled down her calves and bit gently into the arches of her feet.

Discomforting yet generous. She was nude, and could touch herself, but she didn't want that. She wanted to touch Blanca.

Who was ignoring her. Carmen could see her anytime she looked to one side, her gaze wandering up a pair of bare legs stretching onto her, making her a human ottoman. Blanca sat on the couch wearing only a black bra and pink panties. Her beautiful cheeks rose round against her eyes in a self-satisfied smile. Happy with herself, disinterested in Carmen's plight, too busy playing solitaire on the cushion beside her with a weathered pack of playing cards. Her yet-to-be-kissed-today belly hung over her panty line, taunting. Were Blanca to spread her legs, she could show Carmen how transparent the underwear was, how the shadow of hair stretched between them.

She instead kept her legs crossed, feet resting on Carmen's back. Still, something of a fire lit in Carmen between the welcome pressure of Blanca's disinterested touch. The discomforting ropes. The soft cloth wedged between Carmen's teeth.

Her attention narrowed to Blanca's love handles, her arms, her hands twirling cards, and Carmen's fingers twitched between her legs, tickling at curling hairs—no, not that. She could touch herself anytime. She wanted to place her hand instead at Blanca's waist, let her fingers sink in, feel the cool joy of that softness.

And Blanca knew it. She could sense the quivering frustration trembling beneath her feet, swelling through Carmen's entire body, and went on ignoring her.

Ignoring, but consciously so. There was a touch of red in Blanca's cheeks, a heat encircling her, maybe even relief at Carmen's resurfaced lust and enthusiasm. She was excited over the predicament she'd placed Carmen in, but she wouldn't make it obvious. Blanca controlled her own actions and expressions, seeing it all yet giving almost nothing away.

As if the first person Blanca had ever restrained was herself.

Carmen shifted again. Tugged at her bindings. Grunted through the cloth gag wedged behind her teeth and bound around her head. Testing that restraint and control.

"I told you to hold still," Blanca said, gaze locked on her card game of playing with herself. "Every distraction makes this take longer. If you want my attention, you'll have to be patient."

Carmen tried waiting. Watching Blanca find the next card for her solitaire rows. Her smile eased into a smirk, and she leaned over the couch far enough to stroke Carmen's hair, her ear, before pulling the cloth into a loose halo around Carmen's neck.

"What?" Blanca asked in mock impatience.

Carmen smacked her lips. "I miss the ball gag."

"Well, whose teeth ruined the last one?"

A GAME IN YELLOW

"Not my fault. You make an animal out of me. We can't all be in control like you."

"I'm not in control—I'm responsible," Blanca said. "You're the one who's in control. A snap of the fingers." She tapped Carmen's cheek. "Or a dimetrodon, if I let you speak."

"Don't let me speak, then." A sudden severity clung to Carmen's voice. "Don't let me breathe."

Something flickered in Blanca's gaze. Impatience? Fear? Disgust? Carmen lacked Blanca's gift for fluently reading a person's looks, but she wasn't entirely illiterate either.

You'll lose her, Carmen's mind threatened.

Her excitement began to wane again, the flame dying. Paranoia could be a self-fulfilling prophecy if you let it ruin enough parts of your life.

Carmen shuddered, pushing the thought away. "What did I do?"

"Nothing, Pet." Blanca's gaze returned to its usual confidence, and she let out a tiny chuckle. "It's like you can't get off unless someone almost kills you."

"You've never wondered about sex at the edge of life and death?" Carmen asked.

Blanca's chuckle broke into a genuine belly laugh. She pulled her feet from Carmen's back and sank off the couch, onto the floor. "You're too much," she said, pressing into Carmen, breathy, sweating. "And I can't get enough."

Her fingers stroked Carmen's wrist, the touch so light as to be almost imperceptible, licking a sweet jolt along her skin. A game of mischief danced in the dark line of Blanca's smile.

Carmen kissed her, taking in the softness of Blanca's lips.

She wanted to taste where that mischief led. Blanca lunged for a harder kiss, and Carmen laughed into her open mouth. Nothing was so simple as pretending one overpowered the other, but she could still feel Blanca's measured reasoning in this moment. *Kiss, and be quiet.*

Carmen could almost do it. "But that's what Smoke's book does. Makes you feel like you almost died, but you made it, and you're exploding with life. It's an earthquake and a madness."

Blanca leaned back. "You want to see her again, then." It wasn't a question, just another easy read. "Maybe this Sunday, if you like."

"Don't you want your night off?" Carmen asked.

"You aren't work," Blanca said, stroking Carmen's hair. "And I'd do anything for you. Don't you know? I'll take you to Smoke."

"To the book," Carmen said. That was what mattered. If the play were by itself, it would be just as sweet. "Question."

"One."

"Isn't that why you took me down there? You knew what the book would do?"

"Partly," Blanca said.

"Partly you knew?" Carmen asked. "Or partly you had other reasons?"

Blanca hooked her fingers around the damp cloth beneath Carmen's chin. "That's more than one."

Carmen open her mouth to speak again. "But you—"

Blanca wedged the cloth between Carmen's teeth again and then dragged her close, a knotted bundle she could squeeze in her embrace. Gentle fingers explored the bare skin between the knots, and soft lips kissed up Carmen's throat.

A GAME IN YELLOW

"Before *I* satisfy your curiosity, you need to satisfy *me*."

Carmen tried to let that sink in as Blanca grasped Carmen's hands and guided them against the black forest between her thighs. As Blanca shed her meager clothing and pulled one of those thighs between hers.

Paranoia could drown in sweat, be smothered in skin. Carmen only had to let it happen. To find the joy in Blanca's joy.

And it worked.

But it was the last flame her inner spark wheel could manage. The sense of the play's euphoric effect burned away through an orgasmic cry, a survivor having survived too long since her last brush with catastrophe.

A part of her understood there was no survivor's euphoria without risking danger. She didn't really want to go back to Smoke's underground den.

But she needed to. Blanca had found so much joy in this past week—too much for Carmen to dare let her down again. Blanca had tried to be patient through Carmen's many failings, but she wasn't some unfeeling idea of a girlfriend who could weather every pitfall without trouble. She could be sensitive too, interpreting Carmen's lack of enthusiasm as rejection, whether Blanca wanted to or not. It could happen to anyone, but Blanca didn't deserve it.

And damned if Carmen would inflict that on their love life again. Her fire needed refilling before reaching that dismal place she'd wallowed in before glimpsing those tawny pages and their black ink.

She needed *The King in Yellow*.

7

Secondhand Smoke

Act II—Scene 1.

Upon the shores of Hali, the great steps climb forever and endless toward the amber skies above the city of Hastur, above the city of Alar, above the beauty of lost Carcosa, a redundant title, for all places beneath the twin black suns of the Hyades are lost. The sound of brass and wind floats upon great ululations, songs riding the echoes of screaming. They herald the ascent.

Enter THE STRANGER, carrying a great tome, its front as pallid and faceless as himself.

STRANGER   Indeed. It was time.

He stops along the steps and gazes briefly into the black nothings of the twin suns, forever setting. He then opens his tome and begins to read aloud.

～

The shutting clap of *The King in Yellow*'s cover quaked down Carmen's spine. She sat up gasping, feeling like she hadn't inhaled since ancestral fish first crawled from the ocean. Electricity shot through her, and she could've believed someone had hooked her nervous system and blood vessels to Underside's power-siphoning wires. Sweat beaded down her flushed neck, and her button-up clung to her sticky chest. Every inch of skin screamed with quivering desire.

Blanca crushed close beside her, thigh to thigh, bicep to bicep. A warm aroma exhaled from her hair, unfamiliar and irresistible, and Carmen's shallow breath quickened as if to breathe Blanca in. She slid one hand toward Blanca's skirt, patterned with green swirls.

Blanca propped her cheek against her fist, squishing part of her adorable face. "No."

Carmen's trembling hand froze an inch above Blanca's thigh. "No?" she asked, confused.

"Nope," Blanca said, a shrug in her voice. She snapped the waistband of Carmen's black leggings, mischief prowling in her stare. "You got yourself worked up reading that play. Not my problem, Pet. You want to get off? Take care of yourself. Go on, under the table, where nobody's going to see."

Carmen gaped, heart pounding hard, clit pounding harder. She glanced to Smoke as if expecting pity, but Smoke had her chin propped on her palm, black talons drumming her cheek, intrigue swelling in her red-rimmed eyes.

A frail cry of frustration jumped up Carmen's throat, and then she sank beneath the table, into the shadows braced by Smoke's crossed legs and Blanca's open skirt, where her sweet thighs spread, glistening and forbidden. The visual taunt made Carmen shake even worse. Her leggings became a flexible prison, and she reached inside them to stroke a damp divide.

Smoke hummed amusement. "You got her well-trained."

"She's a cat. Domesticated herself." Blanca's hand reached under the table and ruffled Carmen's short hair.

Carmen shuddered at her touch. Part of her wanted to argue. Everything else surrendered to the throes of *The King in Yellow* and survivor's euphoria.

"And like keeping a cat entertained, it's easy some days, less easy others," Blanca went on. "You haven't seen her when she's trying to impress me. It's strange and serious, like she wants to do right by me but wants to challenge me, too. A Carmen that isn't Carmen."

"Like a mask," Smoke said. "Or a mask slipping."

"There's the beauty. I get to have both. I get it all." Blanca's foot tapped Carmen's thigh, urging her closer. "She's been slipping away, but your book's doing the trick for now. We should be paying you."

A rhythm beat through the table above Carmen's head—Smoke drumming her fingers as she spoke. "Money is blasé. I trade in experiences, and right now I'm experiencing the two of you." She paused. "A fascinating experience."

Blanca's legs shifted. "Is trading how you got *The King in Yellow*?"

"Sort of."

Smoke's seat creaked behind Carmen as she kicked off one boot, then another, and then nestled her feet against Carmen's back, again making her a makeshift ottoman.

The weight was comforting, the treatment a thrill. Same as when Blanca had done it earlier this week. Carmen almost bucked against this—she belonged to Blanca; she was *Blanca's* furniture if anyone's—but Smoke's touch sent a cry of delight raking across Carmen's tongue.

Blanca peeked beneath the table. "Callate."

"What?" Carmen asked between gasps.

"You're being rude. Come here."

Blanca gripped the hair at the back of Carmen's head. Her touch was soft at first, a practiced hesitation, awaiting Carmen's assent. When Carmen nodded, Blanca's grip tightened, and she dragged Carmen's head between her legs, under her skirt.

Only then did Carmen discover Blanca's panties were crotchless. A dark nest and tender lips drew her in as if she were possessed by an otherworldly thirst—

Drink deep, the waters of Hali.

—while still stroking between her legs, Smoke's feet still resting on her back.

Glass clinked above, Smoke picking up her vape pen. "The play was a big deal at the end of the nineteenth century."

Blanca muttered a distracted acknowledgment.

"People have tried using it to plot revenge, form cults, usurp monarchs. More than anything, it would get them killed, by others' hands or their own. That dipshit Hitler wanted it, and his occult priests looked for it when the Nazis invaded France, but the French Catholic Church had been working to destroy every copy for the previous few decades." Smoke's heavy exhalation shuddered down to her feet. "They almost succeeded. At least, according to the man who traded it to me."

Blanca let go of Carmen's head, and the table shuddered. "Keep going."

It was a command for Carmen, or Smoke, or both. Carmen pictured Blanca leaning over the table, both arms beneath her, facing down, eyes shut in ecstasy, and that only drove Carmen to taste deeper, stroke harder.

"There was this bazaar in Mexico, couple years back," Smoke went on. "The man there, he told me one of those French priests had found a copy, but instead of burning it, he read it and then spirited it off to Central America. That's where he split it in two before he—whatever the hell happened to him. Act I somewhere, Act II elsewhere. Splitting them up made them safer. At least, *safer* was how I interpreted the trader's words at the time, but my Spanish is shit. He likely meant *less potent*."

"Yeah. Safety first." Blanca sucked in a rushed breath. "If it's French, how come Carmen can read it?"

Smoke chuckled. "This thing doesn't care about human language. If the Tower of Babel were real, whatever's underneath the pages would've stood defiant, a yellow middle finger to God and church alike. Like I said last time, it reads you, too. It makes itself understood."

"Oh." An earthquake rocked Blanca's figure, and her thighs squeezed tight to Carmen's ears, muffling a brief whimper.

Her legs relaxed from Carmen's skull as Smoke's feet slid away, maybe back into her boots. Carmen retreated beneath the table, still rubbing herself. Wasn't anyone going to please her, too?

Smoke hummed again. She really did have a singer's voice. "Don't you reward her?"

"The love is her reward." Blanca again ruffled Carmen's hair. "You relish this, don't you, Pet? You love me?"

Carmen nodded again, rubbing her cheek to Blanca's knee. She did. But she would've loved some attention, too.

"I understand the appeal," Smoke said. "Relinquishing freedom, offering submission, subservience—it's also abdication of responsibility. When you're bound, either to another's will or physically, maybe both, it isn't your fault you aren't finally going to church like you promised, or filing your taxes before the last minute, or arranging a side hustle to squeeze a few more coins into your bank account before rent's due. Someone else keeps you. Might as well enjoy the high of that freedom."

"A role in the game," Blanca said, collecting herself.

Smoke understood less than she thought. There was a contradiction between freedom and captivity, a control in yielding control. Carmen set the boundaries. Blanca facilitated them, and she was careful beyond measure, observant of limitations. She understood perfectly how the difference between a protective fence and a prisoner's cage could be a matter of the submissive's state of mind.

And beneath that mind, there was a comforting darkness, like a subbasement to thought, free from the world's influence and expectation. That under-lizard of the brain, overtaken by desire.

A GAME IN YELLOW

Carmen wanted to tell Smoke this, but she was little more than that reptile side right now, too intoxicated to think straight. Could scarcely pay attention as Blanca pinched her arm, summoning her attention.

"Smoke?" Blanca asked. "Do you want to play with us?"

Carmen listened hard for Smoke's answer, but her side of the table became strangely quiet. She might sit beyond touch as much as she acted beyond money.

Except she'd touched Carmen. It wasn't much of a taste, but she'd taken it just the same.

A misty exhalation slithered over the table. "Okay, I'm game," Smoke said. "But I don't sub. And it doesn't seem you do, either."

Stillness slid into Carmen, a pressure ready to burst. She wanted to get off. She wanted to go home. Blanca's hand came petting again, curious of Carmen's thoughts, inviting a nod or a safeword, either speaking *dimetrodon* or snapping her fingers.

Third partners hadn't been worth the trouble in the past. Carmen had reflected on this herself over a week ago.

But that was before she met Smoke. Before Smoke rested her feet on Carmen's back, a subtly affectionate disregard that thrilled and enticed. Smoke meant possibilities worth exploring.

And more than anything, she carried *The King in Yellow*.

In slow inches, Carmen raised her chin and then nodded twice against Blanca's hand. Her merry fingers danced down Carmen's neck and shoulder, to her arm, pulling her onto the seat. They were going home for their fun.

But not alone.

"No submission, no problem," Blanca said. "Carmen's happy to be shared."

8

The Gameboard

ASCENSION, WALKING, SUBWAY RIDE, MORE walking, more trains—the journey home felt eternal. An ordinary fixation would have eased, but the play's impact had carved impatience into Carmen's heart.

And home brought further delays. Blanca sent Carmen to gargle mouthwash first thing, which could've waited until the night was over. Returning to the living room felt less an intimate invitation and more her cue to get onstage. Blanca should've noticed a disparity, but the additional partner distracted her. She didn't command Smoke, instead taking the role of leader, guiding her to listen for snapping fingers and prioritize Carmen's wellness.

The threesome began with more teasing than Carmen needed. Her body was already worked up, while her mind needed priming. She would've liked to peek at *The King in Yellow* again, study its fragments for lines and stage directions, but Smoke left the book in her satchel. Distance spread between herself and the game, as if Blanca and Smoke were the only players, with Carmen as their gameboard.

She wouldn't have minded that, but her participation felt functional, as much a chore as vacuuming the carpet or washing the dishes, edging toward arousal without truly snaring her. Previous threesomes had been sprints when she'd wanted a marathon. Now, when she longed to rocket toward ecstasy, Blanca and Smoke chose to take their time.

Levity came when they finally undressed. Opposites in shape and tone, Carmen relished the sight of Blanca sliding from her clothes like the sun cresting from storm clouds. Smoke was a tender breeze in flesh, caressing Carmen's hair and teasing sweetness where the head of her member pulsed pink against the inside of her deep blue panties. Carmen hadn't put her mouth around a girl's dick since she first moved to the city until now. Smoke's flesh was soft even when standing, as if every part of her body only knew gentleness.

As the evening drew on, and Carmen came around Blanca's fingers, she realized some of a threesome's appeal. They could do this again, maybe. And they could do it in a way where she wasn't still craving touch by the time the others tired out.

The three of them lay across the living room furniture, TV flickering mindlessness at their disinterested eyes. When Smoke left, and Blanca went to bed, Carmen could satisfy herself. Let the evening's disappointment go. In the soft seat, beneath a warm blanket, she might doze and touch and then sleep deeply. Maybe she would have a kind dream.

A GAME IN YELLOW

But she expected fitfulness. Likely the play's efficacy had fallen down the gap in time between reading and sex. Another glimpse would do her a world of good.

She realized the others were talking, and she'd tuned them out between her thoughts and the vapid late-night talk show. Her attention surfaced to a conversation fragment.

"—more of a hobby," Blanca was saying. She caught Carmen's uncertain look. "Your photography?"

"Oh," Carmen said. "I wasn't listening. Sorry."

"What kind of photography?" Smoke asked.

"The salaciousness kind." Blanca scrunched her nose and then laughed. "I mean, salacious kind. God, my head's a disaster right now. Anyway, she gave it up after a few months."

"When I'm eighty, I'll be glad I have them to look back on," Carmen said.

"Every hobby of hers is temporary," Blanca said. "She was in a band in high school, for a little bit. Played the bass. Never since."

Smoke's eyes glimmered blue light. "Did she wear a dorky tie?"

"She did! The pictures are adorable." Blanca's cheeks turned rosy. "Maybe she'll wear one when she marries me."

"You can be flaky, too," Carmen said, more defensive than she meant to sound. "Remember, you used to be all about nights out at Raspberry Swirl? And then you stopped?"

Blanca scrunched her nose again. "Pet, what are you talking about?"

Carmen studied Blanca—genuine confusion in her eyes. Had she forgotten the club? She'd remembered it last week, and forgetting was out of character for her. More a Carmen thing to do. But then, Blanca had said her head felt off. She must've blanked out on the Swirl.

"Never mind," Carmen said, tittering to pretend she didn't care.

The others echoed her laughter. Carmen studied them, giggling naked together, legs entwining between blankets and the couch. A white misty snake slithered from Smoke's lips. She and Blanca seemed to be playing another game, with Carmen still their gameboard. If they wanted her to keep up, Smoke had the book they'd need.

"Why can't we read Act I?" Carmen didn't mean to blurt it out, but too late to stop it.

"That's where your head's at?" Smoke asked, raising an eyebrow.

"She's insatiable," Blanca said, almost bragging.

"Mm." Smoke puffed her vape. "Don't have it. Like I told Blanca, though you were kind of distracted. Besides, it would do you wrong."

"Do me?" Carmen asked, which made Blanca laugh again.

"Act II is already a hard stab," Smoke said. "But at least your mind can protect itself if you swerve away. But according to the man who traded me the play, Act I—it flays the mind so gently, you don't even notice. All your defenses, gone, and then Act II breaks you with its irresistible truths."

Carmen shifted where she sat. "Is truth that bad?"

"Depends. It's irresistible, understand? Cannot be resisted. That's why I'm a safe guardian for it. The un-tempted." Smoke's gaze seemed to reach kissing distance with Carmen. "But you're a peculiar one. *Do you seek oblivion?*"

Carmen didn't think so. She looked from Smoke to Blanca

and back. Somewhere in the dark of her mind, she wondered if love was a flavor of oblivion.

"That's what the last owner asked me," Smoke went on. "Or how I translated it. But I have another quote for you. *When you gaze long into an abyss, the abyss also gazes back into you.*" She reclined against Blanca and smoked again. "The way I interpret that, the abyss gazes because even an abyss can be lonely. And if it sees you looking, it might start to wonder if you like it, I mean *really* like it, and it might grow fond of you in return."

She looked to the TV with disinterest—not her abyss of choice—and then slid up from the couch and stretched.

"No one's kicking you out," Blanca said. "You can stay the night."

"Rain check."

Smoke stuffed her vape in her satchel and set it by the apartment door. She'd left her tank top dangling from Carmen's seat and had to reach over her to get it, smirking as her breasts hung above Carmen's face.

Carmen glanced up between them and then chinned at the bathroom. "The trains get delayed around our stop."

Smoke tugged on her tank, shot Carmen a wink, and then disappeared into the bathroom, where the light glowed yellow beneath the door. Blanca shuffled to her feet and headed to the bedroom, probably to slide on a robe. The apartment was getting chilly. Carmen had every reason to stay in her seat, nestled by the warm blanket.

But only a few feet away, there lay Smoke's satchel. Unwatched.

Carmen tucked the blanket around her shoulders, tiptoed across the living room, and hunkered down over the satchel.

Its drawstring was loose. She yanked it open and pressed past a spare tank top, leggings, lipstick, vape cartridges, a sleek black shaft that might have been another vape pen, everything piling against the leathery cover of *The King in Yellow*.

Behind the bathroom door, the toilet flushed.

If Carmen tried to read now, she'd miss her chance. She pincered her fingers around the corners of two loose pages in the middle and slid them from between the covers.

The bathroom faucet surged. Clattering followed, likely the soap dispenser falling over.

Carmen tugged the satchel's drawstring tight and tucked the two pages into her blanket. A shuddering breath slid out as she backpedaled. Along the couch. Toward the chair.

"What are you looking for?"

Blanca's voice scraped ice through Carmen's blood. The lust ran out of her in crystalline shards, shredding her muscles to loose ribbons, and she couldn't catch her breath.

"The—" Carmen let the syllable run. "Oh, the remote."

Blanca studied her a moment, hunched on the floor. Forever perceptive Blanca, who could tell Carmen's every alteration of tone, every tick in her expression and body language. It made her a perfect dom but nearly impossible to fool.

"Don't you think Smoke kind of has a Gina-Gershon-in-*Bound* energy?" Carmen asked. "I feel like watching *Bound*."

The randomness made Blanca tilt her head. She approached the couch at a glacial pace, reached over the back, and plucked the remote from between couch cushions as if she'd planted it there on purpose before handing it to Carmen.

"You're too damn funny sometimes," Blanca said, exhausted but amused.

A GAME IN YELLOW

The satchel jostled nearby, and Carmen flinched—Smoke had emerged from the bathroom and was tossing the bag over her shoulder. She hefted it twice, as if weighing its insides for completeness.

Carmen tensed. Smoke couldn't possibly feel the difference in weight of two missing pages. How much could they weigh? Nothing, that's what. They weighed nothing on their own.

Smoke caught Carmen's stare and then approached, lowering herself to kneeling, her eyes boring through Carmen's soul.

"Smoke?" Carmen whispered.

Black talons danced up her fingers. Smoke then lifted Carmen's hand and kissed the back. "See you again, girl."

She headed for the kitchen next, hugged Blanca from behind, and kissed her neck. Carmen did not stop watching her as she made for the door, slid on her boots, wished them both a sweet night, and disappeared into the second-floor hallway. A small dog began barking from a neighboring apartment and then went silent.

"It's too late for a movie for me," Blanca said. A water glass clinked in the sink basin. "Don't forget work tomorrow."

"Yeah," Carmen said, voice shaky. If Blanca asked why she sounded nervous, she could say it was Smoke's tender hand kiss.

She didn't need to know about the pages. Carmen felt at them beneath the blanket with her un-kissed hand, fingertips tracing the tattered edges, enjoying the hidden papery crinkle as they crumpled against her side. She could hardly believe she'd taken them. Less so that they were still here.

But she had. And they were.

9

Only the Self

CARMEN *lowers a glass wine flute, its insides dotted by golden condensation. She recoils from it, communicating without a word that she does not remember drinking.*

    CARMEN   I think it's gone to my head.

CAMILLA *stands beside her, lowering a similar glass from beneath her mask.*

    CAMILLA   It should, my sweet. Who wants to be in her right mind at a time like this?

~

A backache woke Carmen from the dream. She must've curled into a weird position on the couch overnight. The TV's sleep timer had shut it off, but it wasn't Blanca, and it couldn't guide Carmen to bed. Blanca was sleeping in, no café shift today. She didn't need to know Carmen hadn't come to bed.

And she didn't need to know about the stolen pages from *The King in Yellow*.

Carmen had passed out before reading them, but tonight would be her chance. She slipped toward the playroom and nestled the tattered yellows between the mermaid art's frame and the holes she'd stabbed in the wall, and then she hurriedly showered and dressed for work.

The outdoors were crisp, with September finally easing toward autumn, but the train cars were hot, and the office was freezing. Liza had the frustrating habit of leaving the air-conditioning on until November, no matter the temperature. The other women at the office came prepared with cardigans. Carmen would have to try better.

"Late again," Liza said, approaching Carmen's cubicle. "No sandwich?"

"I forgot," Carmen said, plopping her tote bag on her desk. "Didn't get much sleep." Her hands twitched above the keyboard and mouse, eager to clock in before she was any later.

But Liza lingered. "Forget I brought it up. Some arrangements should go unspoken."

Carmen turned to her. "It might sound presumptuous."

"Maybe so." Liza tapped the cubicle wall. "I'll let you get cracking."

The rest of the day came rife with mistakes. Someone had left the coffeepot burning empty in the percolator. Carmen needed to print a report, and naturally the vicious copy machine jammed four times before finally spitting out a wrinkled approximation of text. Needful claws had stolen the cold fries she'd left in the breakroom fridge on Friday.

If only she could leave. Blanca was off from the café but had to bartend tonight. She and Carmen weren't likely to see each other until tomorrow unless Carmen left now.

The pages, Carmen reminded herself.

She would miss Blanca, yes, but stolen yellow treats waited at home. Carmen was allowed to indulge, unless she and Blanca were playing and the rules said no touching herself.

A past conversation surfaced in her memory. Shortly after they first met, Blanca had come home to find her roommate vanished, along with the roommate's things and some of Blanca's. She'd cried and raged to Carmen about it for a weekend, and soon enough they were moving in together. Halfway through installing Carmen in the newly vacated room, they thought better on sleeping apart and turned the spare into a playroom to satisfy their joint interests instead.

They were tangled together in bed, legs trapping each other in a postcoital snare, when Blanca said, *Can't believe I let my family convince me this was a sin.* Seemingly out of nowhere, and yet something grim must have been stirring in her head.

Carmen hadn't wanted to dwell on family troubles. No sense putting Blanca through the pain, and it wasn't like Carmen had wanted to break open her inner crypt, where the lie of her parents' unconditional love had decayed long ago.

You think that's bad? Carmen had asked. *I used to think it was sinful to touch myself. Our church was obsessed with virginal sanctity, like you'd pop your cherry by crossing your legs wrong. It got dark. I wasted so much time worrying and praying. All along, I could've been fucking myself.*

Blanca had squealed with laughter, full-chested and glorious, and then she and Carmen had wound into a tighter knot until dawn.

Where was that joyous Carmen, full of life? Had work destroyed her? Or could she never be satisfied with a good thing? *Temporary*, like Blanca had said last night. Maybe Carmen had quit believing in good things since her parents.

Or since Aja.

Carmen sat up in her seat. What the hell had just fallen into her head? *Or since*—she'd lost it already. Memories washed in of a stormy night, a trashy motel—no, that was Blanca. Except she hadn't met Blanca then.

You're remembering some movie, Carmen thought, reclining in her seat.

Bad enough for the office to kill her spirit; now it was stirring her memories into oatmeal, too.

In the late afternoon, she left her desk to use the restroom, having to head past the breakroom, where a few of her coworkers gathered in a cluster, faces shiny with a smartphone's light.

"He's cute!" one of them cried.

Carmen didn't mean to slow down. Why should she care what her coworkers did with their time? But the two-word outburst carried more weight and honesty than anything she'd heard amid these white walls in some time. She paused to peer through the breakroom doorway.

"Cute?" one woman asked. "Him?" The others joined in, harassing whoever had fired off the positive assessment.

"There's nothing to him."

"With that haircut? Bleh."

A GAME IN YELLOW

"He looks like someone threw him in the washer and forgot about him."

The group cackled together, and Carmen couldn't tell which one of them had unleashed that honest outburst in the first place. Later, that woman would pretend she was joking, but Carmen knew better. She had released a truth, and the others had punished her for it until she surrendered to their collective opinion.

Nothing left to see here. Carmen retreated from the doorway to head for the restroom.

But her movement must have caught their eyes. "What do you think?" one of them asked.

"Yeah, Carmen, tell us."

"Is he cute to you?"

"Come on, you should have an opinion."

One coworker aimed the phone screen at the doorway, and Carmen approached with hesitating steps. She had no idea what other women saw in most men, and this guy was no different. Some celebrity in a backward ball cap and windbreaker. Probably a comedian or an actor.

Carmen shrugged. "I'm not particular about him."

A moment of silence followed, and then the breakroom burst into giggling.

"Oh, wow."

"Is that how you talk?"

"I just love it."

Carmen's hands clawed for pockets to hide in, but of course today she'd worn the slacks without them. These women were in their mid-twenties to late thirties, but they reminded Carmen of high school hostility wearing the mask of a compliment.

Or was she being too sensitive? Blanca could've perceived the truth, but she wasn't here.

"I never noticed a difference," Carmen said. She tried to shrug again, but her shoulders resisted, like this wasn't their problem.

"Very different!"

"It makes you stand out."

"Kind of silly?"

"But also serious."

"Never change it, though. It makes you interesting, and Lord knows you need it if you're going to keep so quiet."

One of Carmen's hands balled into a fist behind her back. "So now you like different? Interesting?"

The women stared at her, some of their brows furrowing.

"You never like what's interesting," Carmen said, and she pointed at one. "Is that blouse one you're comfortable in? Or is that what you're expected to wear?" Her finger aimed at the screen. "Is he what gets you wet? Or is he what you're told to want?"

The others' eyes widened, or blinked, or glanced away. One woman turned the phone to face the group, and its absence at last freed Carmen to go to the restroom like she'd wanted in the first place. This wasn't her scene, and her perpetually superficial coworkers couldn't understand.

None of them would tear their masks away and find the sickly truth beneath. Truth could be ugly, but at least it was honest.

When Carmen left the restroom, the push-button hand-dryer still whirring behind her, she found Liza waiting with her arms crossed over her chest.

"Carmen? I think it's time we have a talk about appropriate workplace behavior."

It took every muscle of restraint to keep Carmen from rolling her eyes. "Okay?"

Liza slipped closer, volume lowering. "Listen, sometimes tempers flare when you stuff too many people in a small office. It's normal. Remember, we're all here for the same reason. But we have to maintain civility." An unsettled atmosphere drifted from her in a sigh. "The time away from the office after next week might do you some good, too. Get to know your coworkers a little."

"You mean the mandatory thing?" Carmen asked.

"Mandatory synergistic workshop, yes," Liza said. "I hear it's pretty in the Catskills this time of year."

"Right." Carmen had forgotten about that. She hurried out the next part, eager to lay her excuse between herself and Liza. "I forgot to mention, but I don't have a car. I sold it a year after moving to Queens."

"Worst-case scenario, you can take a bus and corporate will reimburse you."

Carmen felt a headache coming at the bureaucratic hoops that might entail.

"But I bet someone can give you a ride. I'll poke around." Liza's expression turned smug. "See? It helps to be on good terms, especially if you're in for a couple hours of driving together. Good to remind yourself that we're a team. Try to chit-chat a little more at the anniversary party. It'll help when we're out in the Catskills for the workshop if you show you're willing to make friends. You might even end up more of a team player than you expect. But no more biting anyone's heads off."

A dozen protests rained through Carmen's thoughts—they were all here for a paycheck, nice words could hide knives, saying nothing would have been misconstrued as rude and she would have gotten into trouble anyway, and so on.

But they were ripples on a lake's surface. Eventually, the momentum would end where the water met the land, and none of the disturbance would matter.

"Sorry," Carmen said at last. "The copy machine put me on edge."

"Welcome to the club," Liza said, but her tone softened. "Look, we don't need to like each other. Keep the attitude level, clock out for break if you need to have a cry, and we'll all make it to end of day. Deal?"

It wasn't really a question. Carmen flashed her brightest smile. "No problem."

~

A text hit Carmen's phone as she entered the apartment building. The heavy door thundered shut behind her, closing her in the dim white hall. Aging grime formed orange-brown islands where the ceiling met the wall. Carmen turned to her phone. An unknown number with a city area code.

UNKNOWN: where do u live

Carmen gave the phone a hard scowl. Another text struck before she could think whether to type a reply or block the number.

UNKNOWN: I need to no where u live

CARMEN: Wrong number.

She reached the stairwell's first ascending step before

another text struck. She didn't need this right now, not with a special evening ahead.

UNKNOWN: is this Carmen?

Maybe it was Smoke. Maybe it wasn't. Carmen could ask later. Her thumb jabbed the corner of her screen to open an options tab and then blocked the number. She would ask Blanca if she knew it later.

Carmen made it halfway up before another text rolled in, and the quake of her phone passed a tremor through her upon the steps. No, she'd blocked the intrusive stranger. They couldn't be bugging her with a new number already.

She set her teeth, glanced at the screen, and settled with relief.

BLANCA: Short-staffed so headed in early, and then staying out. Don't wait. Kisses!

That sounded like a long night. Carmen wasn't sure why Blanca needed to parse it that way—out for one shift, and then staying for another?—but she probably wanted to be clear. Carmen shot a quick text back.

CARMEN: Hope it goes quick, love you!

Plus a dozen hearts. She didn't like going to bed alone, but having the apartment to herself, for a particular purpose, knowing there would be no interruption? That sent her grinning up the stairwell. Her keys fell from shaking hands when she first tried to unlock the apartment, and she needed a calming breath before getting on with the night.

Were the pages still behind the mermaid print? Or had Blanca found them, recognized them without reading, and taken them with her to return to Smoke?

Carmen kicked off her shoes and rushed to the playroom.

The pages crinkled as she eased the mermaid's frame from the wall. Perfect. And with only two pages, there was no risk of reading too much without Smoke here to shut the play away.

Time to indulge.

Carmen shut the playroom curtains and lit a pair of tea lights alongside a hickory-scented candle. A soft blanket draped the playroom bench, ready to tug over her body for comfort. She spent half an hour choosing the right music, the right vibrator, and the gentlest binding for her forearms and wrists. Blanca "Safety First" Lugo would have shouted at her for practicing self-bondage alone.

But Blanca wasn't here. That was the point. Besides, Carmen could escape the loose fabric easily. The bondage wasn't her focus anyway.

She had *The King in Yellow*.

The candlelight chased dancing shadows across the playroom as Carmen reclined upon the leathery bench and reached her bound hands toward the pages between her legs. A fire lit within her core and burned down to her curling toes. She was ready. Her eyes shut tight and then opened fast, and she began to read.

There was no setting the mood. She had taken the pages at random, without beginning or end. The play simply persisted mid-act, mid-scene, its existence an in-between.

He gazes down upon the cities, cursed and empty. His hand opens as if willing the Lake of Hali to part its waters and let this stairway descend inside it, but his tome would not survive submersion, and he clutches it in his protective grasp.

A GAME IN YELLOW

Ever-black stars watch like the pupils of a giant as his attention returns to his tome.

STRANGER   Act I—Scene 2d. The girl lies alone in her childhood bedroom. A mother's wailing fills her house, and the girl covers her ears yet cannot shut out the noise.

CHILD   Stop. Please stop. Go to sleep.

STRANGER   She waits and waits for either sleep's embrace or her mother's woe to wane. Usually, she drifts off to that crying, exhausted by its tormented midnight lullaby. But in the day, the sounds haunt her, and she wonders if unhappiness might be hereditary, if she is doomed to this same woe herself. And then she wonders, would her mother know joy if she didn't have to raise a little girl alone? If she was not a mother at all? She wears this un-joy so distinctly that anyone who looks upon her must know her entire tragedy.

THE STRANGER lowers his tome and looks again to the skies, the suns, contemplating and digesting what he has read. With regal clarity, he gives a ponderous observation.

STRANGER   The curse of loving that which is hollow. Of loving Carmen Mancini.

10

Echoes

FUCKING JESUS!" CARMEN'S BOUND HANDS flung the pages toward the foot of the bench, scattering them over the floor.

An eruption in her chest flooded her limbs with fire. She tried yanking her forearms apart, but the fabric had somehow knotted while she read, and she needed to carefully unwind the bindings to get free. The resistance set her nerves alight. She could grab up the still-rumbling vibrator and enjoy the euphoria that she'd been denied last night.

But the playroom teetered with the echo of a mother's wailing. Carmen's yearn-terror tilted into scratchy panic, and that panic tipped her body off the bench. Her knees crashed against the floorboards, stinging up and down her legs. One hand rubbed at her ear, desperate to wipe the aural memory away.

When had she last heard her mother cry like that? Not since that high school fight and that awful night with Blanca.

You met Blanca two years ago, Carmen thought. *Not ten, not fifteen. Not back in high school. Just two years.*

Nothing made sense right now. Carmen tried to get up, but vertigo pinned her to the floor. Her other hand splayed ahead for balance.

Paper crinkled underneath her palm—a page from *The King in Yellow*.

She glanced at it, jaw hanging, eyes blurring as if to protect her from the text, and then she grabbed both pages and stuffed them back behind the mermaid art print.

Black circles flashed briefly from the wall as she set the frame again. Were the holes in the plaster larger than she'd left them? She didn't want to lift the frame and pages again for a better look, only wanted to get out of there.

Away from stab wounds that echoed eyeholes in a mask.

Blanca came home sometime after one in the morning, smelling of alcohol, creeping on soft steps until she spotted Carmen lying across the couch, eyes open, dressed in pajama shorts and tank. Carmen had cleaned up her bindings, vibrator, and blanket, and blown out the candles, like nothing had happened. Only that hickory scent lingered.

"I told you not to wait up," Blanca said.

"Was it a command?" Carmen asked. She watched Blanca's face fall and cleared her throat. "Sorry. That came out more bitchily than I meant. I'm tired."

"Hence not waiting up, gruñona." Blanca slid off her sneakers and headed for the kitchen.

A GAME IN YELLOW

Carmen wriggled to the couch's edge. "How was work?" She wished Blanca would sit down. "Bad?"

"No, I love spending half the night hassled by some guy who keeps ordering drinks he thinks will impress the bartender."

"Now who's the grump?"

"I've earned it," Blanca said. "But Smoke stopped by again. That was nice."

Carmen glanced at the door—shut and locked. Blanca had come home alone. "She's doing okay?"

"She wants to hang out next week." Blanca patted the table. "Like, go out."

Carmen measured this. Not *play* like Blanca had invited last night. *Hang out*. Which meant Smoke probably wouldn't be bringing the book with her, wouldn't be up for hearing about it, and likely still wouldn't notice any pages were missing.

"We were thinking of going to a movie or a stage play," Blanca went on. "And then maybe stopping into Raspberry Swirl for drinks."

Raspberry Swirl. So Blanca *did* remember. And Smoke knew of it, too, if a stop-in was her idea. At Carmen's only visit, a woman she didn't know had tried to pick her up, doll-like, as if she weren't Blanca's already. Nothing had enticed her to return.

"Depends which night," Carmen said, digging for excuses. "I have that workshop thing. In the Catskills? I'll be gone overnight."

"That's at the end of the month, isn't it?" Blanca asked.

Right, Carmen still had time before that particular chore.

"And I have the office anniversary party." Though she realized too late that would take place during and after work hours.

Blanca looked concerned. "We don't have to go if you don't want. But Smoke is sweet, and I think this would be good for us. All of us."

Carmen measured this, too. She was often oblivious, even spacy, but Blanca wasn't the only one who could find clues in the glint of an eye or the lines on a face.

"You like her," Carmen said.

Blanca didn't answer, but her silence said enough. She'd pulled Smoke into their lives to kindle Carmen's desires and maybe found something for herself, too. Carmen couldn't call herself a good girlfriend without trying to make this work.

An immense yawn sent her head rocking back against the couch's arm. She could have fallen asleep here.

Blanca snickered. "Get to bed, yeah? I'll be right behind you."

This wasn't a clear command of the game, but Carmen obeyed. She changed the sheets—overdue anyway—and the new set encircled her in their crisp embrace.

Blanca soon settled in beside her. Carmen rolled over and kissed the softness between Blanca's shoulder blades, and then clung to her as if she were the last standing wall of a cliffside city crumbling into a bottomless abyss.

〜

She remained clingy through the week, into the weekend. Blanca didn't seem to mind, or if she did, Carmen was grateful to be too dense to tell, especially when they hit a rare Saturday when Blanca had off from both the café and the bar. She was trying to watch *Howl's Moving Castle*, but Carmen kept kissing

A GAME IN YELLOW

her neck. And her arms. And then she buried her face in Blanca's belly and closed her teeth around a striped patch of skin.

"God, you're like a cat in heat," Blanca said, half complaining but also giggling. "I've missed this side of you."

That made Carmen sit up and turn serious. "Which side?"

"The side that's happy to exist with me. You've been so tense. And we're both busy."

Carmen studied the faint crow's-feet bordering Blanca's eyes, the laugh lines around her mouth, searching for... what? She couldn't tell. There was an absence here, and she couldn't figure out what was missing solely by looking at Blanca.

"We don't see each other as much as we should," Carmen said.

"But we make up for it, yeah?" Blanca stroked from Carmen's wrist to her bicep. "And when we don't, you don't have to blame your head. It's okay not to be in the mood."

Again, that sense of absence. Carmen wanted to punch herself. She should be able to read her own girlfriend after two years. If Blanca were twinned, one would see through the other in a heartbeat and understand this.

But Carmen couldn't be her. She scooted away from Blanca's side and reached down to pull Blanca's feet into her lap.

A needful stare passed between them before Blanca shut off the movie. "My feet are sore, Pet. Treat them."

Carmen grabbed lotion from the end-table drawer and began to rub Blanca's feet. They were calloused at the heels and pads. Too much time had passed since Carmen last gifted Blanca a foot massage, and she watched Blanca recline, head on the far couch arm, eyes closed, as her thumbs kneaded into the overworked flesh. She wanted to kiss that neck again. That belly. The act of service created a unique style of restraint, her desire to nip Blanca where her chub poked between leggings and blouse now at war with Blanca's command to ease her burdens.

A little trap, set for myself, Carmen thought. She found herself falling into a rhythm, her fingertips working in tiny circles. Almost as relaxing for her as she hoped it was for Blanca.

The ringing of bells draws a veil of ballgown and mask, resplendent gold, across the countenance of—

Carmen's head shot up. They should have left the movie running to keep her attention, or else she might pass out before this loving task was done.

Blanca's foot twitched, her eyes still closed. "Everything all right down there?"

"Mostly," Carmen said. "Do you ever have weird dreams?"

"Everyone does," Blanca said. "Don't we? And all dreams are kind of weird."

"Tell me one."

Blanca blew air toward the ceiling. "I was climbing a ladder. It went on forever and ever, but I had to keep climbing. I felt like if I got to the top, everything would be fixed. Like, the whole world. But no height was ever good enough for the ladder to end. And I got tired, and my hands were sweaty. I slipped and fell. Then I woke up. Hey, not so rough down there."

Carmen found her hands clutching Blanca's foot the way

she'd held on to her a few nights ago, after the bad trip with the pages she'd stolen from Smoke.

"I'm sorry."

"It's nothing," Blanca said. "Just like the dream. I'm probably frustrated about work. Everybody is."

"Did you act out the dream?" Carmen asked.

"Like, sleepwalking?"

"Sure."

"Never," Blanca said. "My older sister used to sleepwalk when we lived in 'Frisco for a little while with my aunt. Vera would march around the house, opening all the doors. *All* of them. Bedrooms, bathroom, cupboards, front door, even the fridge. Tia Eva finally let us put locks on our bedroom doors. Vera wasn't used to that, so when she couldn't get the door open, she'd wander back to bed. The sleepwalking stopped after that. We kept the locks until my first girlfriend—"

Blanca cut herself off. She'd mentioned bits and pieces in the past, enough for Carmen to assemble the puzzle of two teenage girls in Blanca's youth. For both Carmen and Blanca, there had come an eventual severing from their families.

"I sleepwalked a week or so ago," Carmen said, hurrying to steer the topic back where she'd started it. "But I don't think a lock would help."

Blanca's tone went stern. "I'm not restraining you at night, Carmen. Safety first."

"That's not it." Carmen shifted her hands to Blanca's other foot. "I've been hearing things. Might be dream things. In the playroom wall."

Blanca's heel twitched. "Like mice?"

"Not exactly."

"I haven't heard anything. What did you hear?"

"I don't know, scratching?" Carmen said it with a shrug. "Instruments? My mother, once."

Blanca's expression twisted in disgust. "You thought you heard your mother in the playroom wall?"

"Not in real life." Carmen wasn't explaining this right. "I've been having weird dreams since we met Smoke."

"Since she let you read that play," Blanca said.

A warning haunted her voice, and a strange coldness glimmered in her eyes, making Carmen set her teeth. Blanca had taken them to Underside for Carmen's benefit. Complaining about Smoke or the play would only sound ungrateful.

Worse, if Blanca worried too much, she wouldn't only cancel their plans next week with Smoke. She would smash the entire experience with a hammer of *Safety first.* No more yellow aphrodisiac. A ghost of plastic spread across Carmen's face, the thought of losing the play stealing her breath and damning her to desperate attempts at rekindling hers and Blanca's sex life. Failed attempts, eventually leading to a failed relationship.

Carmen scoffed into a laugh. "You know what? I think I tried Smoke's vape, and her weed might have messed with me."

"Oh." Blanca's warning tone slid to softness. "Don't take things from Smoke. She's very particular, probably a special strain. And you're kind of a baby sometimes."

Carmen forced a smile. She didn't want to look like anything was off. Her hands left Blanca's feet, and she crawled up Blanca's legs, kissing between them, above them, and then Carmen dug her head beneath Blanca's blouse and kissed her breasts. With her face hidden, she couldn't give herself away.

A GAME IN YELLOW

Blanca cackled, whipped off the blouse, and wrapped it around Carmen's head, blinding, muffling, and lightly smothering her long enough for Blanca to roll her on her back and start pulling her clothes off.

Carmen wasn't entirely in the mood anymore, but she could play along as something of an olive branch, more of a distraction.

And it worked.

11

The Yearning Abyss

The city of Alar was once an azure paradise, the only one of its kind, a clockwork burg made wondrous in its perfection. Each timepiece governed the rhythm of citizens' pounding hammers, scholarly scrawling, the collisions of wineglasses in toasts. Clockwork perfection synchronized their footsteps, their very breaths. This, until Alar took on the brunt of Carcosa's shattered time and Hastur's resentment of past and future. A broken clock might be right twice a day, but an overburdened one can never mark the sinking of the suns.

You cannot learn this by watching a performance. You must be reading the play.

The city of Hastur is ever the echo of fallen grace, but an echo can linger, and so Hastur has lingered. A broken survivor of a neighboring land emerged from still waters to found his city from otherworldly fragments, a place where ringing birdsong bloomed from crystalline birds and the streets came alive with melody, an aural resonance living in every brick and cobblestone. When the king vanished, its people made the music their servant, their slave, its sole task the harvesting of every hum and whistle and tune, draining the city's spirit and leaving a hollow shell except where the music burns in a harmonic furnace of finite fuel. It will last only long enough for one final masquerade, as if the king only built this beautiful city to shatter it.

This, too, you cannot learn by watching a performance. You must be reading the play.

The lost city of Carcosa keeps its secrets. You cannot learn them by watching a performance, and you cannot learn them by reading the play. But it may invite a player.

The sounds of commotion rumble from the streets of Hastur, only faintly breaching the golden masquerade.

CARMEN	What is this disquiet?
CAMILLA	Revelry. Or chaos. It is all the same.
CARMEN	I see no chaos here.
CAMILLA	Naïve, dear. Any land must echo its sovereign, even those chasing black stars. Look around you. We make merry in rampant excess while hooting and howling swell from the streets. Are

these not the very worms that leave scarring on the skin and fevers in the brain, only done up in masks to hide their true nature?

CARMEN   You said we're not to know. Not until the Hour of Unmasking.

CAMILLA   The truth defies anonymity. I smell their parasitic nature against my will each time my mask lifts too far from my nose. The land, the people—they can't help echoing their dreadful king. Worms and king alike in yellow, crawling from dark places in the Lake of Hali's depths. Its waters have known parasites until that decay took death itself, for there was nothing left to die. Silent stands the city of golden spires across that placid surface. Empty, too, is Alar, one city cannibalized by another. Here in Hastur, we don our disguises to evade such fates.

CARMEN   But we, too, are people of Hastur.

CAMILLA   It isn't the same. Listen to them—they pride themselves on taste, but their tongues and palates are faint. Take Cassilda, for example. Remarkable talent, but unappreciated. They do not know the marvel that walks among them, even when she is unmasked.

CARMEN   You've reminded me of my intended. She's dear to me, but her

	resourcefulness, insight, beauty—unappreciated.
CAMILLA	We are special, then. To be perceptive connoisseurs when the rest, no matter their masks, bear the eyes of swine. But hush, my dear. Cassilda—or whichever guest stares from beneath that hawk mask—makes to sing.

At the balcony, a figure in scarlet aims her beak offstage, where it is known the waters spread and the sister cities stand quiet. She is masked as befits the masquerade, but her voice betrays her identity, whereupon lovely CASSILDA looks upon the Lake of Hali and lets loose her sorrowful song.

CASSILDA	Along the shore the cloud waves break,
	The shadows lengthen
	In Carcosa.
	Strange is the night where black stars rise,
	And strange moons circle through the skies,
	But stranger still is
	Lost Carcosa.
	Songs that the Hyades shall sing,
	Where flap the tatters of the King,
	Must die unheard in
	Dim Carcosa.
	Song of my soul, my voice is dead,
	Die thou, unsung, as tears unshed
	Shall dry and die in
	Lost Carcosa.

A GAME IN YELLOW

When the song ends, CASSILDA retreats from the balcony, to the masked obscurity of the gathered nobles. A handful give restrained applause, but the rest carry on as if there has been no song.

CAMILLA	She is forever in a state.
CARMEN	Aren't we all forever in a state? But tell me, the song is familiar yet unclear. What of this Carcosa?
CAMILLA	A fallen place. We do not speak its name.
CARMEN	But Cassilda—
CAMILLA	To sing it is different. What cannot be spoken may find a home in music.

A shroud overtakes the ballroom, dousing the masquerade's attendants in shadow. Only CARMEN shows clear as she approaches the nearby balcony, lit by the black stars and faint sky.

CARMEN	Look upon the Hali. The twin suns are always setting, yet they never set. Transparent moons haunt the yellow sky, never clear, never gone. A stillness in time.
CAMILLA	(from the shadows) You are loquacious this evening.
CARMEN	Evening summons poeticism. And it is ever evening above Hastur, and Alar, and Carcosa.

HAILEY PIPER

At the cursed city's name, shadowed CAMILLA pats her mask to be sure it covers her face and then turns away from the balcony.

In her place appears THE STRANGER. He does not enter the stage from either side, instead emerging from the gathered nobles as if he has always been here, his figure adorned in a tattered yellow cloak and a pallid mask. His attention aims at the balcony, head tilted as if listening intently. CARMEN does not notice. Her soliloquy persists.

> CARMEN And reaching for those heavens, the sickly yellow spires of Carcosa, like hands for the King in Yellow. They grasp for Alar, too, and perhaps our city of Hastur. Is Carcosa an empty grave of a city, desperate to be filled? Or is it wholly itself and must fill the hollow of its people? For it is said King Hastur knew those lost streets, an apocalypse of a creature crawling from one city's end to another's beginning, which likewise must eventually end, as it was for lost Carcosa.

The shroud fully engulfs the golden masquerade, including CARMEN and THE STRANGER, and the twin suns become black holes stabbed in an apartment—

—wall, shrinking away as Carmen stumbled backward.

Her heels knocked the feet of the playroom bench, and she fell onto its leather cushioning, nearly toppling over the back side. She had returned to this room, apparently in her sleep. She or someone else had parted the playroom curtains, letting city light in through the window.

And someone must have widened the stab wounds in the red-painted plaster. They now stretched across the wall, impossibly never touching and yet broader than an eclipsed sun in the sky. Carmen couldn't be sure how they'd grown. She likewise couldn't guess why she was naked when she remembered going to bed in a tank top and shorts.

But she could be certain she wasn't alone.

A damp otherness behind the wall, within it, reached out from the grandiose stab wounds, their edges dripping as if a lake pooled behind the plaster. Golden snakelike limbs glistened in the city's orange glow.

Carmen patted at the leather cushions, desperate to drag herself to the far side of the bench, make a soft barricade, anything to keep those limbs from touching her.

They draped the plaster in a twitchy nest, and a pale hand followed. A dingy yellow sleeve hung open from the forearm, its underside dark with stains. Another hand grasped the edge of the other hole.

Carmen's vision blurred, fusing the two tremendous openings together. Their combined emptiness made way for a figure in a tattered yellow cloak to come crawling on amber snake tails down the plaster and toward the bench.

One smooth golden limb grasped Carmen's right ankle.

She opened her mouth to scream. To say anything. Her

hand reached down her side, tensed to bat away the slithering intrusions.

Thin hands and snakish limbs chased over her feet and ankles. Her fingers closed around one of the damp limbs, pulsing and solid and warm, its surface the texture of a human tongue.

The pointed tip coiled around her wrist, and then the figure's ragged garments climbed Carmen's body, an enormous yellow maw, its frayed edges wet and writhing. A curious serpentine nest crawled over her thighs and hips, and the world held still around her, waiting for a signal, a sign, the way Blanca had awaited Carmen's approval that second night in Underside before bringing Smoke home with them.

Carmen's vision uncoupled, splitting the fused black holes into twins again. The cardinal wall behind them blanched to a sickly golden sky.

And with the turn of the world, sinking beneath the lake of her lap, she nodded faint assent.

~

Carmen flailed over the floor, gasping hard for air. She managed not to shriek a curse this time, but she felt one pooling in her gut, threatening to sicken her if she didn't at least whisper it. She was dressed in a tank and shorts, same as she'd worn to bed with Blanca. The curtains were shut, exactly as she'd left them.

A cough rattled up her throat, and she half expected the curse to come flowing in a vomit of yellow worms. Exactly the kind Camilla had mentioned.

"Camilla?" Carmen shook her head and clambered up from the playroom floor. "Who the hell are these people?" She eyed the wall for answers and intrusions.

A GAME IN YELLOW

The stab wounds were the size she'd left them when she drove the screwdriver through. She could tell without having to remove the mermaid art print—it had fallen to the floor, chipping the frame's corner but somehow not shattering its glass. Carmen could scarcely imagine Blanca doing that. She doubted even she would bother in her violent sleepwalking.

But what about a presence inside the wall? Something lurked there and had tried to get out, knocking the frame away in the process. Cockroaches? Rats? Carmen had heard of snakes living in people's walls, too, though the snakes weren't usually yellow. She hoped that at least some ordinary animal was to blame. A something, and not a someone.

And maybe someone on the other side thought the same, hoping Carmen was nothing more than a pest.

My older sister used to sleepwalk, Blanca had said. *Would march around the house, opening all the doors.*

All doors. Carmen blinked at the stab wounds. What kind of doors might they be? Portals through plaster? Or somewhere beyond? The wall gave no clues. Its eyeholes stared back with its twin abysses, swollen as if the darkness behind them were a substance prone to yearning and leaking out and grasping anything it could touch.

Carmen broke eye contact, swerving to face left. The movement felt familiar, a stiffening up her spine and a thunder in her blood. She recognized it as she placed the mermaid print back on the wall.

It was the same jolt inside her as when she had to stop reading *The King in Yellow*.

12

The Reptile and the Bird

SMOKE'S STAGE PLAY OF CHOICE for the group outing was an independent production of *The Night of the Iguana*, performed by local college kids to the best of their ability. She said she was a big fan of the writer. Carmen forgot his name and more by the time a cooling September breeze ushered them along the sidewalks and streets, where it stirred dark puddles, echoes of earlier rain. The humidity threatened to snap with another squall before they reached Raspberry Swirl.

"Should we go home?" Carmen asked. "I have an office party after work tomorrow, and it's going to be a long day."

Neither Blanca nor Smoke looked back at her. She might only have thought she'd spoken. Smoke was asking Blanca what she thought of the play, but Carmen caught little of what they said.

She'd caught little of the play, too. It definitely took place in Mexico, but the story lay deceptively distant in memory. More like Carmen had watched the performance a decade ago than minutes earlier, retaining only the vaguest images.

As if her mind had room for only one play, and no others.

Not like the college kids could've tried a production of *The King in Yellow*. They would need the first act. And how would actors memorize their lines without reading from those insidious pages?

Maybe a clever director and stagehands could throw something together before the cast went mad, interrupting readings with uncursed lyrics. That was it—*The King in Yellow: The Musical*. The jukebox kind, cobbling together songs like "Yellow Flicker Beat," or "Goodbye Yellow Brick Road," and even "Itsy Bitsy Teenie Weenie Yellow Polka Dot Bikini."

Carmen's sudden cackling boomed over the street, drawing looks from other pedestrians.

But not Blanca or Smoke. They had stopped short at the corner, where Smoke's black dress wafted around her thighs. The night's shadows seemed to stretch its fabric up her face, reducing her to white eyeballs with two dark centers jittering in confusion.

"What the fuck happened here?" Blanca asked, sounding hurt.

Carmen looked at the building ahead. She had only vague memories of Raspberry Swirl's appearance—a small stage at the back, round standing tables, a row of booths, a bar. Every indoor surface had glowed blue, while the outside swirled with pink neon, and the door was painted black. You kind of had to know what the place was before you got there.

Not anymore. Glass windows revealed a golden-brown

A GAME IN YELLOW

interior, as if someone had hollowed out a giant rotisserie chicken and jammed a bar and restaurant inside. The stage was either gone or built over, the walls adorned with baseball and football paraphernalia, license plates, and other knickknacks.

Gone was any hint of a BDSM club thriving on this site. The name above the glass doors instead read Rico's.

Blanca's phone glowed in her hand as she scrolled for info, a stream of curses growling under her breath.

Smoke peered over her shoulder. "It shut down?"

"How could this happen so fast?" Blanca let her arm drop. "Nobody told me."

She hadn't visited Raspberry Swirl in months, but she spoke like she'd stopped in after work just last week, only to find everything different now. Time must've passed without her noticing. Out of character for Blanca, but not impossible.

"The city changes quick," Carmen said.

"It must've been a buyout, or some rezoning bullshit," Smoke said, shaking her head in disbelief. "That's not right. You can't suck the soul out of the city and replace it with—emptiness. With *this*."

Except you could. Maybe it wasn't right, but you could do it. Carmen almost said they were lucky this was still a site where people gathered, even if not the same people. It could be worse. Someone could have established a cubicle-cluttered office for advertising or data entry. Soullessness came in many flavors.

Given the chance, entire chunks of the city might someday decay into urban versions of Carmen's hometown, possessed by a stale apathy that reached inside and overtook you.

Everywhere would feel like the past. Like the office. Dead inside.

"Carmen?"

The voice startled her. She turned, half hoping it had been Blanca with a frog in her throat or Smoke speaking at an odd pitch, but in mid-swerve, Carmen recognized an intruder. This voice did not belong with her after work hours. It should have stayed in the office, where she'd last heard it. She hadn't been sure whose it was then, lost in the communal giggling, but now she could pin the voice to a particular outburst.

He's cute! And later, *But also serious.*

A group of four women emerged from Rico's corner-facing entrance. One lithe figure broke from them. Strawberry-blond hair bounced around a toothy smile, pointed nose, and large blue eyes that wandered up and down Carmen, as disbelieving of her as she was to see this woman here. She'd been in the breakroom at work, ogling that guy on another coworker's phone. The one who'd dared offer an independent opinion about him.

"Oh," Carmen said. "Hi."

"It's wild to run into you," the coworker said. "I've been trying like hell to get ahold of you."

Carmen couldn't remember any such thing. "My phone's been weird."

"You live around here, don't you?" The coworker glanced around. Her thick eyeliner made her eyes look deep-set in her pale face. "I'm in Astoria, and when Liza gave me a Queens address, I was like, phew, that'll make everything a breeze."

"Everything?" Carmen asked.

The coworker pursed her lips and then opened them. "Yeah, for the party. We have the big motivational seminar thing, and then the office anniversary party? If you get loaded,

A GAME IN YELLOW

I can help you home." The coworker gave Carmen's arm a playful punch. "Designated commuter buddies."

Had Liza explained this to Carmen? Maybe the explanation lay in an email she'd ignored. She wasn't supposed to have to think about work right now.

"I had you pegged for a Staten Islander," the coworker went on. "You're always rushing out like you got a longer commute than the rest of us. Thank God that's not the case. Maybe we'll be carpooling to the Catskills by month's end if you play your cards right."

Before Carmen could ask what about her had given a Staten Island impression rather than Flushing or somewhere else distant, Smoke cleared her throat in a rising set of notes, as if readying to break into song. Blanca nudged close, her smile brighter than the streetlights. An insistence burned from her eyes—she wanted Carmen to make introductions.

Except Carmen didn't know her coworker's name. Only Liza mattered as supervisor, and maybe whoever appeared as representative of whichever company had most recently purchased the office, but those names came and went.

Who was this woman? Were her friends also Carmen's coworkers? No, the gaggle of barhoppers were strangers waiting at the curb, ready to cross the street but unwilling to abandon their friend. Out-of-towners? They wouldn't know where to go next without Carmen's coworker. Lost outside of their usual habitat—Carmen could relate. The meeting of office life and private life filled her skull with lead, threatening to drag her to the sidewalk, where a concussion could plant her back in the golden masquerade.

Smoke brushed toward Blanca's other side and set a hand on the small of her back. "Hey there. I'm Smoke. This here's Blanca."

The coworker gave a little wave. "Natasha. Carmen and I—we're at the same office."

"Neat," Smoke said, and then she cocked her head toward the sports bar. "How's this place? Any good?"

Natasha craned her neck and studied Rico's with those large eyes. "No clue. We just popped in for pregaming before the club. It's not bad, I guess?" Her uncertain expression burst into beaming. "Hey, do you all want to come with? It'll be *fuuuun.*"

She sang the last word, and Carmen shrank inside, desperate to hide behind Blanca.

Move on, she thought. Enough dullness had overtaken the corner without the office encroaching on her time off.

"Don't we have work in the morning?" Carmen asked.

"I won't get hangover loaded, promise," Natasha said. "And the party isn't until after work. I can handle myself, and we can hang out more then."

"We can hang out then," Carmen echoed. Her gaze flashed to Natasha's patient friends and back.

Natasha took the hint. "Yeah. Then."

She rejoined her gaggle and led them across the street, light chatter climbing from between them, but Carmen couldn't make out any words and didn't want to.

More than anything, she wanted tonight to be over. They'd planned to hang out with Smoke—done. Mission accomplished.

"We're going home now?" Carmen asked. "The Swirl is gone and—"

A GAME IN YELLOW

She stopped herself. Would Blanca and Smoke understand that a coworker's presence made for a bad omen?

"We can get drinks here," Blanca said. "This isn't too different from where I work, and your coworker seemed fine with it. I'm just—" She let a deep breath shudder out of her. "I'm disappointed."

Carmen studied her. Blanca must've taken the club's presence for granted, thinking she could come back anytime and it would be waiting for her. Instead, it was leftovers gone moldy in the fridge.

When Carmen looked to Smoke for guidance, she found empty sidewalk. Had Smoke followed Natasha? No, Smoke had already gone inside.

Blanca started to follow, but Carmen slid her arms around Blanca's shoulder and waist, drawing her into a tight embrace. She returned the hug and said nothing. Too proud to cry over a place she'd abandoned months back, but she needed a little love anyway. Affection would have to make a consolation prize over explanation. They might never know what had become of the Swirl.

When they drew apart, Blanca kissed Carmen's cheek. "Cheer up. We'll make the most of it."

Rico's had none of Underside's arcane atmosphere, but Smoke looked at home beneath the dim golden lights. She'd already secured a back-end booth plus a trio of water glasses and a basket of bread by the time Carmen and Blanca joined her. Her satchel and dark jacket lay crumpled in the seat at her side.

"This place is too typical," she said. "Couldn't they have at least installed a gimmick restaurant if they had to replace Raspberry Swirl? Or a gay bar?"

Blanca squeezed deep into the booth, across from Smoke. "That would be too much character. Damn sure would've scared Natasha's friends away while she was talking to us."

"They keep closing the gay bars anyway," Carmen said, eager to rush the conversation past her coworker's intrusion. She didn't want to think about work, or the party, or the mandatory workshop at September's end.

"There and then gone?" Blanca asked, despondent.

Carmen planted herself at Blanca's left. "It would've turned into this place eventually."

Smoke hummed a low note. "The rainbow drought."

Her eyes fixed on Carmen as she raised a slice of buttered bread to her lips and eased her teeth into it, savoring the view, the taste.

A waitress in white appeared, asked if she could set them up with drinks or appetizers. Carmen stuck with her water while Blanca and Smoke each ordered something stronger, along with nachos and artichoke dip. The waitress jotted the order down and vanished.

"One night at the Swirl," Blanca said, heady with reminiscence, "I was with my friends. There were these two women—never learned their names—one was a squishy girl like me, and the other had mountains down her arms and legs and back. She went to work suspending the other woman with this system of weights and counterweights, and these red ropes splayed out from her in all directions, like she was a spider bound at the center of her web. It was breathtaking."

A bad taste skittered over Carmen's tongue. She bit down to keep from saying anything she'd regret, but Blanca's remembered awe made Carmen wish they were home.

"Soon enough, there won't be anything worth knowing in this town," Smoke said. "At least on the surface. Every interesting place will burrow underground, and you'll have to know somebody who knows somebody to have a neat time. The rest—carrion for the tourist birds. Maybe Carmen was right. We should've gone back to your place. Something about this bar makes my skin itchy."

"We could go now," Carmen said.

She didn't miss Raspberry Swirl like Blanca and apparently Smoke, but it at least had a serene atmosphere. Rico's held a twitchy unease, an atmosphere of writhing insect larvae that spread from the chatty drinkers on barstools and the blasting television above them.

The sounds of commotion rumble from the streets of Hastur.

"Don't encourage her," Blanca said to Smoke, and then she gave Carmen a playful shove. "She never sticks anything out. I told you about her old hobbies right? Photography lasted, what, six months? And she told me she quit that high school band in three. I forget how long she took up coding, but that's done, too."

"She's eclectic," Smoke said. Fascination beamed from her bright eyes.

"Have you always lived in the city?" Carmen asked, eager to change the subject. She set a bread slice on a small plate in front of Blanca and then took another for herself.

"A year, so far. I tend to drift." Smoke aimed her diamond-inked and club-inked fingers in a V across the table. "You two?"

"I'm from out west, Carmen from the Northeast," Blanca said. "But we met here, like, a couple years ago."

"Yeah, I know out west, too," Smoke said. "Wandering between Oregon and Mexico."

"When you found the book," Carmen said.

Smoke scratched at the table where scraps of a straw's paper wrapping had been fused to the wood by condensation. Her gaze darted toward the bar, avoiding Carmen's eyes. Tonight was not the night to bring up *The King in Yellow*.

"Pet." Blanca smirked. "Quiet."

Carmen spread her hands. "What?"

"Nothing," Blanca said. "But be quiet for a little so Smoke and I can have an adult conversation."

Carmen bristled. That wasn't fair. She hadn't wanted to come here in the first place, whether it was Raspberry Swirl or Rico's. Her fingertip and thumb pincered. She could break Blanca's command with a snap. As far as she knew, they weren't supposed to be playing tonight.

But maybe she had it wrong. Smoke's expression burned with intrigue, as if there were no better way to get her attention than for Carmen and Blanca to play their game. It was almost exhibitionist. Was that Blanca's new thing? Exhibition could be Carmen's thing, too, if she let it. She didn't exactly mind that blazing look in Smoke's eyes.

The waitress returned with the drinks and nachos. When she left, Blanca slid the bowl toward Carmen. Her pincered hand opened and closed around a nacho's tip, and she took a bite, her gaze not leaving Smoke until she swallowed.

A silent flirtation of eyes and food—she could play that game, too. They could all play.

"So," Blanca said, propping her chin in her hand. "How long were you in Mexico?"

"About a year," Smoke said. "There were a couple trips to line things up for an operation in Mexico City, and then I lived with an ex-friend in Mexicali after. That's where I fell hard for this woman Relena."

Carmen perked up, and Blanca leaned in, curiosity buzzing between them.

Smoke rubbed her lips, smearing pink gloss on her fingertips. "She was older than me. Her husband was gone, and her sons had started some business together in TJ. Her brothers were around, but she was somebody who hadn't given much to herself in her whole life. And she wanted to eat me. Her words—couldn't get enough of my skin. We were all over each other.

"My friend didn't like it, though. I left the bedroom door open by mistake once when Relena was over, and I found out later he watched her climb on me in nothing but her red skirt, foot on my tit, teeth at my ear, rubbing herself all over me. And after Relena left, he told me we were grotesque. Fetishistic. I couldn't explain then how she was hungry like someone who's been starved forever. So I told him I was sorry no one had ever wanted to get in his skin like no touch was ever good enough. He slapped me in the mouth and kicked me out that day. I think now he believed we were something we weren't. Never felt that way for him, though. Relena decided to end it before something bad happened, and I came back to the States."

A quiet settled over the table. The waitress slid by to ask if they needed anything else, and they shook their collective heads.

"Sorry," Smoke said when she left. "I didn't mean to offload."

"We asked," Blanca said. "We want to know you."

Carmen nodded. She and Blanca were no strangers to grim

pasts full of people who had cut them away, or had given them little choice but to do the cutting themselves. If Smoke was severed from such a past, maybe Blanca was right and she belonged with them.

"Ladies! Good evening."

Their heads turned to the booth's opening. A man stood watching them, almost expectant, and Carmen wondered briefly if he might be a manager checking if they were having a good time.

But then she caught Blanca's sudden stiffness, reading the man before Carmen could. He was a barfly and must've been watching them, working up the nerve to approach their booth. Doubtful he'd expected a three-headed lesbian monster to glower his way.

Carmen chewed another nacho, staring, assessing. Plain features, skin pink by complexion or drink, a nothing-to-write-home-about haircut, no style to his clothes, his facial hair, his uncertain posture. No aspect of him stood out in any discernible way.

He looked exactly like the kind of man the women at the office would fawn over.

"I couldn't help but notice you're without manly companionship," he said. His hands burrowed into his jacket pockets, his forwardness turning timid at the last second.

"Why do you think that might be?" Smoke asked.

Blanca gestured to Carmen. "We have a masc."

Golden dreams flickered in Carmen's head—no, not a *mask*. Blanca had been referring to Carmen as if she were a tiny masculine trophy wife.

A GAME IN YELLOW

The man raised a hand out of his jacket. "Name's Roddy, hi. I know I'm intruding, and I know guys aren't allowed to waltz up like this anymore."

"Yet here you are," Smoke said in singsong.

Roddy nodded.

Smoke aimed a claw. "Let me guess. Usually when it comes to getting a girl off, you're Mr. One or None, but sometime in the recent past you managed to get her to a second coming, and now you think you're Jesus."

Roddy slumped into a hunch. He seemed to be reading the room now, and Carmen almost felt sorry for him.

"Is this the part when you tell me to fuck off?" he asked, monotone.

Smoke reached into her satchel and lifted the sleek black shaft Carmen had spotted while stealing pages from *The King in Yellow*. It didn't look like another vape pen in the light. Smoke's finger hesitated along its side, a deep breath before a dive, and then pressed a switch, freeing a serrated blade from the shaft's top.

"Usually this sends the same message," Smoke said, dancing the switchblade over her tattooed fingers.

Carmen watched Roddy's eyes widen in shock, but he didn't slink away. Maybe he thought relentless determination made him special. Or maybe he wasn't thinking at all.

"Put that away," Blanca snapped. "You'll get us kicked out."

Smoke flashed Roddy a smirk and then stuffed the switchblade away. Roddy held his ground.

Blanca waved an upturned palm toward the bar as if presenting prizes on a game show. "Let's play a game. We like games here. You make out with one of those fellas at the bar for thirty seconds, and"—her gesturing hand found the back of Carmen's head and gripped her hair—"I'll let you have fun with this one."

The outer walls beyond the booth dimmed around the golden light above her. *The shadows lengthen in Carcosa.*

Blanca's grip turned Carmen's head toward the booth's inner corner, where her deep-set gaze pounded a promise into Carmen's thoughts. Everything would be fine.

Roddy shifted on his feet and then scoffed. "You're screwing with me." His matter-of-factness sent Blanca and Smoke cackling, and their joy drew him looming over the table's end. "What are you thinking? Gay chicken?"

Blanca blinked up at him. "Gay chicken?"

"You know, same kind of chicken as when two cars are rushing at each other?" Roddy asked. "See who's the chicken and dodges? It's like that, except guys' lips instead of their cars. Used to play that in college."

"Did you win?" Blanca asked.

"Sometimes."

"Well, Roddy, girls don't do that."

"Right," Smoke said. "We just kiss."

A grin broke over Roddy's face, but to his credit he managed not to go *Hot* or *Sexy*.

"See, your problem is, you don't appreciate the beauty of your fellow man the way we appreciate each other's beauty." Smoke flashed Carmen a look she couldn't decipher and then reached across the table to touch Blanca's arm. "See her? The curvature of her, and the way the light casts her shadows like a sunset. A daily miracle."

The twin suns sink.

Carmen shook the fragment of dream away. Fresh desire

A GAME IN YELLOW

crept beneath her gut, hotter than any sun, thinking of Blanca, of Smoke appreciating her the way she deserved. That was good—everyone should know her specialness. Her beauty, and cleverness, and joy.

"Smoke," Blanca said, waving a bashful hand.

"And this one," Smoke went on, sliding her hand toward Carmen and tracing claws across her fingertips. "Imagine her wearing rope. A gift to see it nestle and contour into her softness and then loosening to paint patterns across her skin. In the heat of that moment, you could taste her in the air. And that profile? Those angles? There's art in the way the light slides down her face, accentuating each feature."

Carmen blushed. Smoke had never seen her tied up, which meant Blanca must've told stories. Vivid ones. Enough to muster curious visions in Smoke's head.

"That's cool," Roddy said, like Smoke had described the weather. "You got a fixation, I guess."

"And a vexation." Smoke's hand retreated to her side of the table. "It isn't enough you can't appreciate your fellow men, but you don't appreciate women either. You probably like that they gutted the carcass of a beautiful place and stuffed it with this flavorless bar. Enlighten us, Roddy. What do you look for in a girl?"

"The usual." Roddy shrugged. "Tits, ass, the right waistline."

He could not be sober and blurt that out. Carmen rolled her eyes. Not only would her coworkers like him; he would probably like them, too. Why even approach this booth? None of their trio of women fit his ideal. He was purely hungry and would take anything right now.

"That's regurgitation," Smoke said. "You don't know yourself or the beauty around you. We exist on two entirely distinct planes of reality. By some happenstance of dimensional liminality, we're meeting in once–Raspberry Swirl, currently Rico's, and after tonight, we'll go our separate ways. You live in a wasteland and demand it shape you a rose. We live in a garden. There's splendor everywhere we look and touch."

Smoke stood and bent across the table and kissed Blanca on the lips. She then craned toward Carmen, her intense eyes seeking permission.

Carmen flashed a glance at Smoke's lips to give it. Smoke's kiss landed quick and hard.

"Fuck," Roddy said, impressed.

"Yeah," Smoke said, dragging her words as she eased back into her seat. "Fuck."

Carmen took a deep breath. "We—"

Blanca flashed her a warning look, and Carmen shut her mouth. She hadn't been given permission to speak, and she wasn't about to interrupt this game.

"You like playing chicken?" Smoke said. "The kind more dangerous than a kiss?"

Roddy went quiet as Smoke opened her satchel, her talons clicking down the front of a leatherbound tome, one Carmen had been sure she wouldn't get to see tonight.

The King in Yellow.

Her limbs stiffened, and thunder boomed in her chest. She wished she'd taken the inner seat where she could tuck into the booth's corner, but the best she could do was crush herself against Blanca's warm softness.

"This is kind of like chicken," Smoke said, turning the volume toward Roddy. "Who will dodge first—the boy or the

A GAME IN YELLOW

book? If the book dodges first, you get away. If you don't, it keeps you."

"Not that," Blanca said, amused. She started to pull the book back toward Smoke. "She's kidding."

But Smoke held the book firmly against the table. "I'm not. Kidding." A mirthless humor slid into her tone. "The man wants to play, B. Let him play." She moved her satchel and jacket onto her lap, making room for Roddy to sit beside her.

He didn't hesitate. "Yeah, sure. I'm not chicken."

"Sure, you braved coming over here," Smoke said. "You want company. No harm done. Even an abyss can be lonely."

Roddy looked into her eyes. "What?"

"Nothing. Roddy, do you know how a stage play is like a game? If you win, I'll tell you." Smoke batted her lashes. "And then I'll reward you."

"And if I lose?" Roddy glanced over the table's nacho bowl and mostly full drinks. "I'll cover your bill."

"If you lose, it isn't going to matter." Smoke cracked open the tome.

Carmen caught Roddy's gaze. He'd braved coming over here, yes. Would he bravely plow through the play's pages? Smoke would have to stop him before he reached the missing section.

"The short one," Roddy said, chinning at Carmen. "She doesn't talk?"

"That one isn't your game." Smoke tapped a yellowed page. "This is."

Roddy eyeballed the top of the page. "It's a play?"

"What else do you do with a game but play it?" Smoke asked.

A smile curved into Roddy's cheeks as he shook his head and began to read, eyes sliding over one line, then another. Carmen could half read the upside-down beginning to Act II.

Upon the shores of Hali, the great steps climb forever and endless toward the amber skies—

Carmen stopped herself before the play reached its fingers into her thoughts. She'd never watched someone else read the book before. How would Roddy react to the onset of survivor's euphoria when no one in this booth wanted him? Maybe he would rush into the bathroom. Or head home. Carmen only hoped he'd go away.

But Roddy turned the page and began to rock from side to side, his shoulder bumping into Smoke's. She ignored him, watching, waiting. Her gaze never touched the page, curious about all things except the text in the tome she carried.

"Smoke," Blanca said. "You usually stop Carmen before this."

"True," Smoke said, disinterested. "But he isn't Carmen."

Roddy rocked too far toward the outside of the booth and tumbled out, onto the floor. A few patrons at a nearby table hooted as if he were some drunk too sloshed to walk straight, but he teetered to his feet, a foreboding look yellowing his eyes.

"Oh," he muttered. "It was a sign."

"Somewhere between terror and madness lies ecstasy," Smoke said. "Or is it that somewhere between terror and ecstasy lies madness?"

Roddy didn't hear her. He glanced around as if lost, and then he stumbled away. "I should have recognized. Should've seen. There's so much to do."

A GAME IN YELLOW

His voice faded into the bar's dull roar, and then he disappeared behind other patrons, out the door, into the city and the night. Carmen opened her mouth to call after him, but she wasn't allowed to speak. What had he meant by "a sign"? And what was going to happen to him?

Smoke clapped the book shut. "Guess you win again, old friend."

⁓

A light rain began shortly after Blanca and Smoke burst out of the bar in an uproarious fit, their voices crackling together as the drizzle met them. Carmen ambled behind, every step cautious. The others drank too much, dizzy and haphazard, but Carmen felt hypervigilant. She studied the water-spotted sidewalk and wondered if Roddy had walked in this same direction.

Her attention snapped up at the sound of a sloppy kiss. Blanca's lips, breaking from Smoke's, and then bursting into laughter again.

"Come home with us," Blanca said, loud against the rainfall.

Smoke eyed her and then cocked her head back toward Carmen. "Let her talk again."

"Oh, right. Pet, you can talk now! We're taking Smoke home with us!"

Carmen had forgotten about the command. Her silence came not from Blanca, but from a wet heaviness in the air, closing plastic-like over her mouth and throat. This was not the same city she'd walked with Blanca and Smoke before stepping inside Rico's. Some vague and invisible element had changed, skewing the color of the light, the texture of the gentle raindrops. Maybe Smoke was right about overlapping realities, united by dimensional thinness within the bar, and they had exited into the wrong one.

Whatever the reason, Carmen had nothing to say.

Blanca didn't notice. She clung to Smoke as they traveled homeward. Briefly they blurred in Carmen's sight, the streetlights casting water-skewed rays around them, and the golden glow fused both women into one amorphous shadow.

Carmen rubbed her eyes, looked away, looked back. She didn't want to see them like this. Didn't want them to echo her dream of stab wounds meshing into one great abyss and welcoming a yellow nightmare into the world.

But that nightmare lived in Carmen's eyes. The nearest streetlight's aura fractured around Blanca and Smoke the farther they walked and the harder the rain fell, its glint forming a tall yellowy veil and a golden crown.

They kept moving up the sidewalk. The mirage should have followed them, but instead it lingered in the air the way a bright light left an afterimage when heading into the dark.

Like someone else had briefly stood with them at the curb and remained watching as they drifted away.

13

The Hyades

THE APARTMENT BUILDING HAD BECOME a strange land. Its first floor's rust-colored grime had paled to mustard, and the stairwell stank of rain as Carmen followed Blanca and Smoke up to the second floor.

Home felt no less strange. Carmen had barely locked the door and slid out of her shoes before Blanca seized her middle and drew her back toward the couch, where Smoke had curled into a grinning ball.

Of course they wanted sex. They were rain-soaked and sloshed and silly, and moreover they'd been making bedroom eyes all night. None of them would reach the bedroom, though. These two didn't simply want to sleep together.

They wanted to play.

Blanca guided Carmen onto the couch's middle cushion,

up against Smoke, but she didn't sit with them, instead standing over them as if waiting for a cue. Some direction from offstage.

Carmen shut her eyes. Forced them open. Blinked several times. Each instance her eyelids lifted, the apartment living room remained, with Smoke beside her, Blanca above. Carmen wasn't reading or dreaming. She was here, at home. Blanca was coaxing Carmen into something unspoken yet understood, and she was letting it happen. That was the core of the game—trust. Most of it in Blanca, but a little in Smoke, too.

Nerves alight, Carmen watched Blanca stray from the couch and disappear into the playroom.

Smoke uncurled one limb from her body and plucked her phone from her satchel on the floor. Her left-hand fingers danced over the screen, flashing her tattoos, each digit a wild card.

"You're looking for music," Carmen said. "Like Blanca does."

"No one seduces anyone anymore," Smoke said, never taking her gaze from the screen. "People think it's too much effort, so they don't bother. They think that magic is gone, like everything about a person should be boxed into checklists, profiles, these little contracts." A low hum radiated from her phone, and she set it down on the coffee table. "But the magic comes when you put in the effort. Mind into matter, will into flesh. Wouldn't you like to be seduced?"

"Okay." Carmen didn't think. Hardly felt capable of thought. Had the others been the ones drinking, or was it her?

Blanca returned from the playroom moments later carrying a line of thin white rope. Red nebulas clouded her eyes. Smoke must've pulled out her vape since leaving the subway and Blanca had taken a hit.

A GAME IN YELLOW

Between the weed and the alcohol, should they be trusted to tie Carmen safely? She didn't know. They both looked to have left caution at Rico's, something their waitress couldn't exactly find and return when cleaning up tables tonight.

Blanca guided a pale loop under and then over Carmen's arms, encircling her wrists, and then offered the rope's tails to Smoke. She tucked the rope between and pulled, squeezing flesh together. A shudder worked through her—she'd never done this before, had she? Carmen would have to be the rock here, holding completely still while she let Smoke work other knots down her forearms toward her elbows.

"A little intense," Smoke said shakily.

Had Carmen ever seen her so unnerved? She didn't think so.

"This is rookie level," Blanca said, a laugh in her tone. "She can reverse prayer better than a backward priest."

Smoke was probably supposed to laugh, too—Carmen almost did. Blanca wielded one kind of rope with her girlfriend and another, less-tangible kind with Smoke. Rattling breath snaked up her throat, sounding both impressed and aroused. Maybe she had a little submissiveness in her after all.

And if Carmen noticed it, then Blanca had seen it, too. Perhaps before tonight.

Smoke pressed Carmen's bound wrists back toward her chest and slid a hand onto her thigh. Each movement was a gentle touch, as if Carmen had bones made of stiff wire that Smoke meant to arrange as a biological statue. One hand crept to Carmen's face, tilting her attention inch by inch toward Blanca as Smoke's mouth neared Carmen's head.

"Blanca?" Carmen whispered.

"Quiet, Pet," Blanca whispered back. She neared the couch and cupped one hand over Carmen's clasped knuckles. "I'm here."

A strange serenity drew tingling across Carmen's skin as Smoke's teeth found her earlobe. Her jaw. Descending to her neck, where her tongue wrote her name into the sensitive dip near Carmen's throat, one slow letter at a time. Her teeth came again then, scraping at first, and then catching Carmen's skin between them. Smoke's jaw worked in steady bites, her face pressing harder against the gap between Carmen's neck and shoulder, hungry to take her in.

The play flashed through Carmen's thoughts, taking her in.

And then her thoughts melted into a breathy quake and a bite of clarity—Smoke might not be here solely for Blanca. She might have come for Carmen, too. Might even *like* Carmen. Want her. This sudden hunger was too much like Carmen's furious desire for Blanca to be coincidence, dripping molten heat down her muscles and boiling a sudden moan up her throat.

Smoke's hand squeezed Carmen's thigh and slid it toward her. She then uncurled herself over Carmen's leg, planting a knee in the cushion between Carmen's thighs, hard against the seat of her pants, and Carmen couldn't help grinding into Smoke's leg. Her lips parted, her head dipped toward Smoke, and she set her teeth against Smoke's shoulder.

"No, no," Smoke said, as gentle as her fingertips nudging Carmen's head back. "I bite. Not you."

Blanca clicked her tongue. "I have just the thing."

She made another trip to the playroom, and Carmen thought she heard rummaging. She couldn't be sure. She was making too much noise herself now, and a line of electricity seemed to be thrashing down her center, finding its spark against Smoke's thigh. Her teeth clamped around her tongue. She needed to stop herself from speaking the notion at the back of her throat.

You make me feel the way the play makes me feel. The apprehension. The need.

"Got this before the last rent hike," Blanca said, returning, her gait uneven, something black dangling from her hands. "We haven't used it in a minute, but she's always liked it."

She nudged past Smoke, who leaned over but didn't remove her leg from Carmen, and the black thing in Blanca's hands settled over the lower half of Carmen's face, covering her mouth and nose with a leather snout. Straps encircled the back of her head, binding the pup mask in place.

"No more biting," Blanca whispered.

Carmen nodded. Another moan rippled through her. She couldn't imagine what it sounded like to the others.

They didn't seem to mind. Smoke was biting Carmen's neck again, and Carmen went on grinding her leg. Blanca's fingers found Carmen's bound wrists again and tugged forward, first lowering her hands to Smoke's thigh, and then Blanca nudged Carmen's head down, and forward, until the snout could nuzzle between Blanca's legs, against her groin.

"There she is." A sigh erupted through Blanca's lips. She'd been waiting for this. "My good Pet. I missed this."

They formed an odd tangle of limbs, Carmen sitting, Smoke kneeling, Blanca standing. Carmen let her eyes shut again. She let her hips quake against Smoke's leg, arms immobile, letting those teeth work at her neck while Blanca grinded against her snouted face. Always for Blanca. Everything Blanca deserved.

The shape of it all turned soppy around her. Carmen forgot

what the apartment looked like, what Blanca and Smoke looked like. Where they were, who they were—none of it mattered.

There was only this exquisite feeling. This mounting fire and lightning inside her.

Her eyes slitted open. She could pass into a void like this, inhabiting a realm made up only of sweet voracious touches, her will a forgotten burden, but she wanted to drink in the fuzzy nearby edge of Smoke. The glory of Blanca.

She didn't look so inebriated anymore. Her form was stern. One hand lay on Carmen's head, keeping her close. The other stroked between Smoke's shoulders. Her hips rocked against Carmen's face. She expected Blanca's eyes to be closed in the same reverie Carmen had dipped into.

But Blanca's eyes remained open. Almost vigilant. She was watching with the patience of a spider waiting for her web to tremble, this moment being the culmination of some grand design.

Carmen was not the only *pet* here. Blanca had folded her control of self into giving Carmen and Smoke an expectant place in this pleasure, crafting a hierarchy of submissiveness and domination. Almost a delegation of command.

As if she couldn't handle Carmen alone and now needed Smoke's help to carry the weight.

A girlfriend who was both not enough and too much.

Carmen tried to speak, but the pup mask muffled her too much for whispers. Her eyes narrowed again, begging for that void where only sensation lived. If she let herself sink into the moment, she could forget this new understanding of Blanca, pawning her off onto Smoke. Carmen could just enjoy the both of them. Go along with everything, thoughtless behind her mask.

Maybe this was the face she wore at the golden masquerade.

The thought sent her jolting against Blanca and Smoke. She took a deep breath, head teetering to one side.

"Dimetrodon," she whispered. And then again, loud enough to power through the leather: "Dimetrodon."

Blanca's grip loosened from Carmen's scalp. "That's it. Stop now."

Smoke's teeth relented without a word, and her knee uprooted from the middle couch cushion, leaving an absent ache between Carmen's legs. She didn't care. The moment drained away as easily as her enthusiasm from before Smoke had introduced *The King in Yellow* to their lives.

Blanca nudged Smoke aside and swooped in to work at the straps behind Carmen's head. "This is what I was telling you about."

Carmen scowled unseen. They had been talking about her? Saying what? She couldn't ask right now, too out of focus even as the leather snout slipped loose from her nose, mouth, and jaw.

"What did she say?" Smoke asked. "Die at the metro?"

"Dimetrodon," Blanca echoed. "The spoken safeword. I forgot to teach you." Her fingernails plucked at one of the knots running along Carmen's forearms. "This is what I mean about the sub calling the shots."

Carmen pursed her lips. She might decide whether or not to hit time-out, but she placed the circumstances and herself in Blanca's control each time they played. The game made for a complicated dynamic. Perhaps too intricate even for someone as smart as Smoke. It lit a prideful fire in Carmen's chest that she could wrap her head around a complexity that maybe Smoke could not.

Smoke tapped a nail to her lips. "Why die—dimetrodon?"

"Carmen's choice. A word you wouldn't typically say during sex." Blanca hurried the rope from Carmen's forearms. "Unless we ever roleplay prehistoric animals, but we'll cross that bridge if we come to it."

"Safety first," Carmen croaked. She rubbed her forearms. They didn't hurt, but her hands needed to be sure she was free.

"Pobrecita," Blanca said, checking her over. "Are you feeling sick?"

It would have been easy to say *Yes, take care of me*. Even understandable, forgivable, for her to ruin the evening with wooziness. A spark writhed between Smoke and Blanca, hot enough to burn without Carmen. Blanca might enjoy a night of sexual nourishment with someone less broken, someone different, and Carmen could kill that joy by playing on Blanca's better nature.

She instead rose shakily to her feet and kissed Blanca on the forehead. "I need to lie down. You deserve a nice time."

A sober Blanca could have read Carmen's face easier than any book, but her eyes were bleary, hands uncertain, and she knew it. No choice but to take Carmen at her word.

"All right." Blanca retreated from the couch, giving Carmen room to scoot by.

"We'll fantasize about you," Smoke said.

If she'd spoken in a mean tone, a mask of friendliness

hiding hostility like the women at the office, Carmen might have changed her mind.

But Smoke sounded like she would genuinely miss having Carmen bound and watchful and wanting. Carmen didn't glance back, only retreated with a faint wave on her way to the bathroom to wash up and then to the bedroom.

Her eyes caught the playroom in passing. Its door hung open, and she half expected an uncertain figure shrouded in yellow to slither from its darkness.

There was no one. Carmen had returned the mermaid art print to the wall, damaged corner and all. Nothing should crawl loose, at least not without knocking the print down again.

I knocked it down, Carmen told herself. *In my sleep*. There was no one else, wasn't allowed to be anyone else.

Carmen reached the bedroom, haunted by her nameless doubts and scrambled feelings, where she closed the door, threw her clothes to the floor, and plucked an edible from the nightstand on Blanca's side of the bed. Weed made her paranoid sometimes, but not when she used it for sleep.

And drugged thoughtlessness might distort her dreams too much for the golden masquerade.

She slid between the sheets to zone out rewatching *Walking with Monsters* on her phone. It was a favorite documentary, unpeopled and easy. The human race was only its fish and lizard ancestry without traceable bloodlines, hardly a twinkle in a forgotten eye.

She'd hardly started before needing to skip ahead. Earth of four billion years ago wore a toxic yellow hue. She skipped again at the prehistoric giant scorpions three and a half billion years later, their shells an unpleasant mix of sun, sand, and darkness. And then she skipped too far, to a pair of dorsal-finned mammal-like reptiles—the dimetrodon itself—animated with yellow-green skin or scales.

At last, she started the video again, set the phone beside her, eyes closed, and waited for Kenneth Branagh to describe the coming of Paleozoic life and lull her to sleep.

This is—

⌒

—the Hyades, a star cluster of untraversable distance, wherein the spaces between unknowable lights dream yellowed unreality upon the Lake of Hali, upon Hastur, and Alar, and lost Carcosa, each in their fashion awaiting the twin sunset with longing and dread. CARMEN looks to the balcony as if someone beyond calls to her, but her name is not among the sounds of Hastur or the golden masquerade. Only when CAMILLA takes her arm does her attention return, and yet her thoughts drift to another land.

CARMEN   There is a legend where I come from, where the king's soul affects his kingdom's life.

CAMILLA   Oh?

CARMEN   Arthur of Avalon. A good king until his downfall, and a good kingdom until then, too. Once his time was done and the throne corrupted, the land reflected the shattered spirit of his world. I wonder, is that the nature of King

A GAME IN YELLOW

	Hastur and his city of Hastur? A shared name must bind a king even tighter to his land.
CAMILLA	You and your strange fantasies. Arthur, Avalon, Aja.
CARMEN	(in whispered confusion) Aja?
CAMILLA	Never you mind. Dread Hastur is a mystery, and the city no longer knows him.

Again, THE STRANGER emerges from the crowd, looming with CASSILDA on his arm.

STRANGER	But there is talk of an heir.

CARMEN places a hand at her chest, elated against her understanding at the appearance of this newcomer.

CAMILLA	(affectionately to Cassilda) You have been social tonight.
CARMEN	An heir?
CAMILLA	Perhaps he is among the masked? He might be the true king of Hastur, or perhaps another city. A king of the beyond, of the black stars, wearing the guise of yellow.
STRANGER	His mantle.
CASSILDA	Charming, isn't he? And a rogue's talent for amusement. See how he dresses. See his mask. The King in Yellow! Few would dare.

CARMEN	I mentioned that title before. It came into me unbidden, like a sudden shortness of breath. Who is the King in Yellow?
CAMILLA	(laughing) You know better than I.
CARMEN	Why?
CAMILLA	He is the one you answer to.

The masquerade fades to black, and then brightens to gold again. For a blink, every mask has dissolved to facelessness. And then the black takes over again, and the gold returns, and the masks of animals again disguise noble faces. Or perhaps they are beasts upon beasts.

CARMEN	With the suns ever-setting yet never set, there is no time. How, without time, do we reach the Hour of Unmasking?
CAMILLA	Alar keeps the minutes. More than one city can be lost across placid Hali. And there are more ways than known in Cassilda's Song to lose a city, a self, a soul.
CASSILDA	Yes, dear. Trust us—the Hour of Unmasking nears.

~

Carmen lifted her eyelids to face black eyeholes.

She held stiff, forehead hovering an inch from the playroom's wall. Her gaze descended the red plaster to her hands, clinging to textures she couldn't immediately decipher in her post-dream weariness.

One hand clutched the mermaid art print. The frame's broken corner aimed at her gut like a knife's edge.

Her other hand clutched yellowed pages.

"Carmen?"

A floorboard creaked behind her, and she turned to find Blanca standing in the playroom doorway, a soft robe hiding her nakedness.

Carmen's hands twitched to drop the frame and pages, but there was no point. Blanca had seen.

"Did I wake you up?" Carmen asked.

"We weren't asleep," Blanca said. "You came naked out of the bedroom like you were practicing a dance. We called out to you."

"About Cassilda's Song?"

Blanca screwed up her face. "Who?"

Smoke appeared behind her in her bra and underwear. She looked exhausted, a tension working through her shoulders as her chest rapidly rose and fell.

"What's that you got?"

Carmen set the mermaid art onto the wall again. There was no point in trying to hide the pages. Blanca left the doorway, giving Smoke a better view of Carmen.

"Are those mine?" Smoke asked. "You went into my bag?"

If only she would pull out her switchblade. Stabbing Carmen in the gut would be easier to withstand than exposing her theft in front of Blanca.

Smoke reached Carmen and plucked up the pages. Her eyes widened. She then placed them back into Carmen's hand and retreated, her brow furrowed.

Blanca peered down at the pages and then glanced at Carmen. "Where'd you get this?"

Carmen at last looked down. If she shot herself with a dose of survivor's euphoria, maybe she could please Blanca in the way she'd wanted earlier, and they could forget this betrayal of taking pages from Smoke in the first place.

Except the first page was not one Carmen had read before. Only now did she notice there were more than two pages pinched between her fingers.

These were not Smoke's pages. She could tell from the very beginning, where four words cleared the air.

Act I—Scene 1.

Carmen's skin buzzed, nervous and inquisitive. Act II was dangerous all by itself if read too far, but Act I was the seductive scalpel, its tantalizing mundanity lulling its reader into a false sense of security. Act II could make zealots. Act I and Act II together could make something else. Carmen glanced over the top, the play laying out a cast. Camilla, Cassilda, other characters.

"Carmen," Blanca said. "Where'd you get this?"

"I found it," Carmen said, thankful she didn't have to lie. "When I woke up."

Smoke shifted back, scrutinizing the room with danger in her gaze. Ever curious, she surely wanted to see what these new pages could do, but Carmen doubted she was willing to create the result herself. More likely she would wait for someone else to find out, a Roddy-like opportuning, and then she could learn from their mistakes.

"Think I'll head out," Smoke said, returning to the living room to gather her things.

A GAME IN YELLOW

Blanca whined after her. "It's late."

"I've walked meaner places at night." Through the doorway, she flashed Carmen a distant look. "When there's something you want to do, but you're afraid to, it must be nice for someone else to give you no choice, huh? I wonder what that feels like."

Did she mean Blanca? Or *The King in Yellow*? Carmen didn't respond, let alone ask, only watched Smoke shimmy into her dress and throw her satchel over her shoulders. She kissed Blanca on the cheek, waved a hand at Carmen without looking, and then slipped on her wet boots and left the apartment.

A haze overtook Carmen's head. She must've absorbed the edible at last. Another dream might hit her soon unless she could stay awake all night.

The wall stared into her. She was almost relieved to know she wouldn't be coming home right after work tomorrow, the anniversary party keeping her late. The extended distance from the playroom might be good for her. No time to hang out with Smoke or obsess over her yellow play.

Carmen only wished she could bring Blanca with her.

Blanca vanished long enough to lock the apartment door and then returned to the playroom, her posture sagging. "I'm brushing my teeth and getting to bed," she said. "You should come, too."

"In a minute," Carmen said.

She watched Blanca disappear again, listened to the bathroom door shut, and then leafed through the pages. Not to read them, only to understand. They looked to be a sizable portion of Act I.

Only at the end of the stack, beyond where Act I cut off, still incomplete, did Carmen find the stolen pages of Act II. They had sat in her hand the entire time. And like a lizard growing back a lost tail, they might have regenerated much of Act I.

How much more of *The King in Yellow* would they grow?

14

Happiness

THE STRANGER turns a page, and his voice brings truth to a world's hollow, reading to un-lives upon derelict shores and the echo of a scream that has itself become a beast.

STRANGER   Act II—Scene 1. A mask of Blanca has been grown, or carved, and placed upon a memory. It is nonsensical, contradictory. A monument to failed forgetting. There must instead be a demonstration of truth, upon which Blanca formed on an opposite coast, and so could not be part of Carmen's youth. There must be a scene of breaking.

The stage of stairways falls dark and then fades into a dim terrace, lit only by outdoor bulbs aswirl with tiny insects. There is no wind, and the air itself is a roiling soup, clinging to the skin of every player.

Enter BLANCA in her early twenties, opening a front door in this San Diego suburb. She presses a hand to the screen door, its mesh bowing beneath her palm and straining a hole where a moth considers an entrance while Blanca considers an exit.

Enter MOTHER. A short woman with wide brown eyes, she is close enough for the outdoor light to reach her.

Enter FATHER. He is scarcely present within the lighting, more comfortable in the shadows of the house, letting his voice do the walking for him.

And enter CARMEN. She is not present, not truly. She is only a watcher, perhaps through a window, or the eyes of one of the swarming insects. Not present, but she can see things she's never been shown, and understand things as if they're being said in a language she speaks, and within all of that, she learns that BLANCA is a runner.

    CARMEN   Like me.

CARMEN isn't certain why she makes this remark. Not yet. Perhaps it isn't real, and that is why it makes no sound upon the scene.

A GAME IN YELLOW

MOTHER	You won't go anywhere.
FATHER	That is the door of the family, girl. That is the door of God. You do not walk away.
BLANCA	(whispering to herself) You won't cry. Never cry.

This moment is not an island but the end of a long peninsula BLANCA has been chasing for time untold. A litany of complaints stir from the lightbulb-obsessed insect swarm, memories and echoes billowing hot in the gloom.

MOTHER	(disembodied) You don't need this. You're so beautiful, my girl, you could have any man you want.
FATHER	(disembodied) When will you let this go? When will you wake up?
MOTHER	(disembodied) Your aunt blames herself. I blame myself.
FATHER	(disembodied) You can't even get married. What is the point?

The echoes fade, and the present voices surge as strong as an earthquake tearing fissures through BLANCA, through her insides.

MOTHER	You want to break my heart, Blancita. You want to kill me.
FATHER	You are hurting yourself, also. Do you think you can find the light of God out there? Where is it? In your home.

MOTHER	Who will give it to you? Your family. A woman cannot show you that. There are men and there are women, and we work together.
MOTHER	Listen to him.
FATHER	And listen to God.

BLANCA clenches her teeth and presses deeper into the screen door.

BLANCA	Fuck God.

The door thrusts open, spilling BLANCA from the house as FATHER launches from the shadows. He is a patient man, and there is much he will tolerate, but not this.

CARMEN	Run! Run!

BLANCA dashes into the street faster than he can catch up, the screen door crashing before he thrusts it open again, but he's too late. She's too far away for him to catch, for her parents to hear this one last cry she promised herself she wouldn't let out.

But she is not far enough away to keep the words of her MOTHER from catching up instead.

MOTHER	(shouting) Where you go doesn't matter, child! You will never feel whole if you don't find a man to give you babies! You will never be happy!

A GAME IN YELLOW

It is something of a curse, following young BLANCA into the night. She won't believe it. She will find work in another part of the city, of the state, and save up, and cross the country to New York, where she hopes to forget the heat and shame of San Diego.

But nothing in life is easy. Her father might have wished to beat her bloody that night for her blasphemy, but it is her mother's words that leave bruises and scars.

~~

The new pages haunted Carmen into the morning, the commute, work. The end of today's shift brought the much-warned-about anniversary party for the office's most recent sale from one company to another, and corporate had sent someone to speak with the team, as if the upcoming workshop wouldn't be bad enough.

Carmen couldn't place his purpose, whether he was a motivational speaker, a chastisement incarnate, or a clown in a business suit who thought he was Alec Baldwin's badgering, roaring character in *Glengarry Glen Ross*.

She could only tell that he was unimportant and not worth listening to. He gathered her, Liza, Natasha, and the rest of the cubicle dwellers into a too-small conference room Carmen only saw once a year when it was time to renew company health insurance plans, where they sat and listened to a speech about a team-building mentality in a place where there was no such thing as a team. He was readying people for management as if a data-entry office offered upward mobility. Carmen and her coworkers were never going to climb out of their cubicles. They would either find new jobs with better pay and benefits, or worse ones, or stay planted here until their eyes dimmed, their wrists took on permanent carpal tunnel, and their fingers arthritis'd their way beyond corporate usefulness. Nothing ever evolved here. The company had changed hands six times in the past four years, each time bringing new orientation meetings and expectations, only for Carmen to trudge through the same data-entry work as always.

She let her mind drift to *The King in Yellow*. What would it be like for the Stranger to stand in this suited man's place, arresting the attention of all gathered?

He would never descend into this drab gray corner. His was a place of music and legacy.

Except in that last part Carmen had read. Or dreamed. She was having a hard time telling the difference now. Sleepwalking might have given way to sleepreading. Or perhaps there was no difference between fiction you read and fiction you dreamed.

Unless it was real.

What Carmen had seen of Blanca felt real enough. The heat of it, the bugs, the crashing screen door, the pain in Blanca's voice. She had never shared any such memory. Carmen only knew she never spoke to her family and rarely mentioned them. And she knew Blanca cried in her sleep some nights, the only state in which she couldn't maintain total control of herself.

The play might be learning about the people around it, impossible as that sounded. Or that scene of Blanca and her family might be as fictional as all the other scenes in the play.

Could Carmen trust it to tell the truth? It might only be showing her what it thought she wanted.

But if what she'd seen was true, what else could *The King in*

A GAME IN YELLOW

Yellow show her? After Smoke left the apartment, Carmen had stuffed the pages into her bag for safekeeping, where neither Smoke nor Blanca would easily find them.

Carmen could read from them right now if she were alone.

The motivational chastisement clown eventually concluded with something about go-getters, told everyone to give themselves a round of applause, and then clung to Liza as they all headed for the breakroom, where someone had crammed pizza and salad.

"I'll just have a little."

"Oh, it's from Ayisha's?"

"Where'd this Chicago-style one come from?"

Weeks ago, Carmen would've laughed. All that buildup, and the anniversary turned out to be yet another pizza party. It was probably corporate mandate, the office slotted into a rung of the company hierarchy designated for a particular level of celebration. Or maybe they were spending too much money on next week's out-of-town workshop. The numbers had to add up, at least until whenever they sold the office to another company.

Instead of laughing, Carmen sighed with relief. A pizza party was nothing, especially at day's end. She could hang around for an hour and say she'd put in the right amount of participation.

Maybe she could find a way into Blanca's past, either through talking to her or by reading again from the possibly omniscient play.

Carmen was headed to eat at her desk when a figure appeared beside her and jammed something cold against her arm—Natasha, clutching a can of beer. A grin lit her face, reaching up into her eyes, where the reflection of fluorescent ceiling lights shined whiter than her teeth.

"Want to make this party fun?" she asked. "I've had one already."

From the smell of her breath, she'd had more than that, but Carmen only smiled back. "Sure."

Natasha set the can on Carmen's mousepad, covering the hole Carmen had stabbed through it a couple weeks ago. One wrong swerve of the mouse, and the can would topple over.

"I know a secret," Natasha said. "I realized it today, while that guy was talking. Ready?" She leaned closer. "Corporate doesn't know what we do here."

Carmen let the idea swirl in her thoughts. "That can't be right."

"It can. It *is*. I'm serious." Natasha thumbed over her shoulder to the breakroom, where the motivational clown's chatter rang through the door. "That speech was for salespeople. They don't know we do data entry."

"No." Carmen blinked at her.

Natasha cackled a beer-smelling laugh. "They don't know they bought a data-entry office! That's how little what we do matters. And the whole workshop thing? In the Catskills? It's going to be a whole-ass waste of time. Except whatever fun we get up to out there, just us girls." Her grin widened as she crossed a finger over her lips and teeth. "Don't tell."

She wandered off, staggering a little, and Carmen's gaze returned to the desk. That corporate didn't know theirs was a data-entry office sounded far-fetched, but Natasha was right about one thing—nothing they did here mattered.

A GAME IN YELLOW

Maybe it took drinking for some people to realize that. If so, Natasha had probably spread her aluminum cans of wisdom elsewhere in the office before she reached Carmen's desk. There were others who would be more receptive to her alcoholic treats. Likely she'd assumed this would be a real party and had been pregaming again. Tonight would see her return to the bars. Perhaps Rico's.

The thought summoned the sports bar into Carmen's head, along with everything that had happened there. Roddy, who'd read from *The King in Yellow* at Smoke's behest. Blanca's little game. And before that, the stories they'd passed around, like Smoke's tale of surgery, recovery, and severed relationships in Mexico.

That was not her first story told to Carmen and Blanca. Not even her first about visiting Mexico. The play had wound up there, after all. Smoke was a nomad.

How far had she traveled? And to which places? Carmen couldn't know, but she doubted Smoke had spent her entire time out west stirring up trouble south of the border. She could've traveled to Texas, Nevada. She'd certainly roamed California. Perhaps even San Diego.

And despite the size of that city, Carmen couldn't rule out that Smoke might have met Blanca there sometime before she moved east.

Where they could have reunited by chance here in New York.

And now what? Smoke had seemed a temporary third, except she wouldn't leave. Would she ever leave? Blanca had mentioned the rent going up in a few months. If they cleared out the playroom, they could sublet to Smoke. Maybe even put her on the lease in January. Blanca and Smoke, together like they might've been before, with Carmen reduced to a third wheel.

Then again, could Smoke's stories be trusted? She might have gone to Mexico for surgery reasons, or she might not. That whole tale about an ex-friend—no one could confirm its veracity. And *The King in Yellow*? Only Smoke could say where she'd genuinely found it, or if it had found her instead.

Why show it to Carmen and Blanca? Surely others had crossed Smoke's path in her subterranean drug den. Perhaps there were other people like Roddy, stunned out of their minds by what they'd read. Smoke might have been seeking someone who'd take to the play.

Someone like Carmen.

For what purpose? To help her learn the truth about Blanca? Hundreds of millions of people across the world had to have relationship problems worse than Carmen and Blanca's. Why help one little sapphic couple in Queens and not everyone?

Don't assume benevolence, Carmen warned herself. *Don't assume anything. You don't know Smoke. You might not even know Blanca.*

But she could learn. Tattered paper stroked her fingers as she slid her hand into her tote bag. She almost didn't want to look.

She couldn't help it. *The King in Yellow* awaited, alluring in its frightfulness, no matter how many pages it'd grown.

And it *had* grown more since last night. Carmen's finger folded the corner of the opening page to Act II, what she remembered as describing the Stranger's ascent of crisscrossing

A GAME IN YELLOW

steps overlooking the Hali and the black suns, fragments of the Hyades.

Enough time with her, and those stolen pages might grow the entire play. Was it really like a lizard regenerating its tail? Or was *The King in Yellow* like a starfish, each severed limb healing into a new whole? The French priest who had split his copy several decades ago might have only helped replicate it. Smoke's Act II might keep growing Act I, and maybe she'd been burning the pages to keep this king from regaining any crown.

Or was Carmen special? She couldn't know for certain, but her curiosity was a hungry animal in her mind, eager to taste the new material.

She tried to skim without really reading, keeping herself from falling headfirst into madness, fantasy, or survivor's euphoria. Despite the number of pages, the descriptions and dialogue moved briskly. She recognized an unfolding of a masquerade, the presence of a stranger, a looming disaster, all of it flowing by as if Carmen had read it—

Dreamed it.

—before. But she hadn't experienced the entirety, and her heart had crawled into her throat by the time she slowed enough to absorb anything.

CAMILLA	You, sir, should unmask.
STRANGER	Indeed?
CASSILDA	Indeed it's time. We have all laid aside disguise but you.
STRANGER	I wear no mask.
CAMILLA	(terrified, aside to Cassilda) No mask? No mask!

Carmen stuffed the pages deep into her bag. She couldn't keep reading here. A few lines of dialogue weren't enough to boil her blood anymore, but if she kept going, she would put herself in an awkward position, and she didn't want to head home and surprise Blanca this way. Better that they do that together.

And what was the alternative? "You can't masturbate in the office," Carmen whispered, smirking to herself.

"Why not?"

Carmen started in her seat, twisting up to find Natasha's grin again. She hadn't heard her return, too lost in her thoughts to notice the pizza party drifting around the office. The motivational speaker stood by the water cooler, still chatting at a disinterested Liza. Other coworkers looked to be checking their phones in small clusters. A few of them clutched beers—Natasha's contribution to the party.

And Natasha was clearly drunk. "Come on. You have to have done it sometime."

Carmen couldn't find the words. Only shook her head, found her phone in her bag, and hoped she could feign getting an important text with strong enough acting to fool an inebriated coworker.

"Never?" Natasha asked.

"Never," Carmen said.

Natasha studied her. "You're telling the truth. But be real, you must've thought about it. Even Liza's done it. Slip a silver bullet in your purse, sneak into the ladies' room, make the workday a little more bearable."

Despite herself, Carmen guffawed. "I'd never want to enjoy the office like that." But now, she couldn't help considering it.

And she wondered if Blanca might instruct her to do it someday, if she asked.

"You know what's better than masturbating for free?" Natasha asked. "Getting paid for it."

Now they both laughed. Carmen let her phone slide deeper into her bag, brushed fingers against the play's pages again, and let the laughter slip away.

Natasha hooked around the cubicle wall. "I'm noticing something about you, Carmen. You get wistful. Ever been treated for depression?"

Carmen stiffened. "I'm not depressed. I have nothing to be sad about."

"It isn't sadness," Natasha said. "Mental health is so not simple. Or, it's even simpler? I don't know. But it's like brain chemicals getting mucked up, disconnected, apathetic, nothingness inside you." She wobbled, and her hand sank onto Carmen's shoulder for balance.

Carmen tried to shrug her off. "That sounds entirely opposite of me."

But Natasha rambled on as if Carmen hadn't spoken. "My sister had it. *Has* it. That's the thing, it doesn't really go. It pretends to. Great pretender, those mental issues. She was diagnosed at fifteen, got meds, got better. Five years later, got worse. Upped her dosage, better, time passed, worse. Changed her medicine, better. And that's the important part! Getting better. People always want a miracle." She banged a can against the top of one cubicle wall. "But progress is two steps forward, one step back. Forever. And nobody likes work."

A shape writhed beneath Carmen's thoughts. Nothing she wanted to acknowledge.

She tried shrugging Natasha off again, succeeded this time, and stood from her seat with her bag. An hour must've passed by now, and even if it hadn't, she wasn't being paid for this. She had no reason to stay and every reason to go home, try to read, maybe talk to Blanca. If Smoke was there—well, she'd cross that bridge later, but she wouldn't come for it. She would even suffer the playroom's nearness if it meant getting away from this corporate hellhole.

"Mancini."

Carmen paused mid-stride at the sound of her last name. No one ever called her that. She turned to find Liza approaching, one hand grasping Natasha's bicep.

"Carmen, I've been saying your name over and over," Liza said.

"Sorry," Carmen said, softer than she'd spoken to Natasha. "I was off in my head."

"Can you get in your head and do me a favor?" Liza guided Natasha to Carmen's side. "You two live pretty close to each other. Take her north, will you? Make sure she gets home safe."

Carmen glanced from Natasha to Liza and back. Swallowed what she wanted to say. Nodded. One hand opened the office door to guide Natasha into the hallway, toward the elevator.

The other gripped her bag against her side, where yellowy pages crinkled beneath her aggravation.

15

One Does Not Belong

ASTORIA SMELLED OF CIGARETTES AND weed as Carmen led Natasha down the clanging steps of the Ditmars Boulevard station stop. She'd had to pass her stop to get here and supposed she might as well walk home after.

It would be an easier stroll than the one she had to make now, with Natasha clinging to her side. They made for a clumsy creature together, sometimes three-legged, sometimes four, depending on how deeply Natasha leaned her weight onto Carmen. How could anyone get this loaded on cheap office beer? She might have been playing it up as an excuse to escape the anniversary party. If so, Carmen wished she'd thought of it first.

"Which way?" she asked.

Natasha slung an arm around Carmen's neck and pointed east. "Home." It came out in a strange giggling drawl.

Her weight sank onto Carmen's shoulders, and they nearly spilled onto the curb as they crossed the street beneath the railway. Natasha was leading but also inhibiting.

"You're such a mess," Natasha said, giggling again. "You can't carry me *and* that stuff. Give."

Before Carmen could stop it, Natasha had yanked away her tote bag and slung it over the same arm as her purse. Carmen flinched to take her bag back, but even a drunk Natasha could be right. The bag's changed position provided a simple counterweight. Walking her home became easier.

They turned at the next corner and followed a street of small houses wedged between larger ones carved into makeshift apartments. Black iron fencing glistened with dew in front of a few driveways. Natasha steered left without warning toward a fleet of chipped concrete steps leading past a parked SUV, probably her landlord's. She wrestled opened the outside glass door, leading into a small brick room, where a golden bulb shined over a steel inner door.

This had to be the place. Carmen could take her bag, leave Natasha here, and head home. Hopefully the next train wouldn't take too long. If so, she'd walk after all.

Except Natasha fumbled her keys, and when she finally got them in her hand, she kept missing the keyhole and scraping the edges.

Carmen placed a steadying hand over Natasha's wrist and guided the key inside.

"You're good at that," Natasha whispered. Another giggle. "Better than a man."

Carmen stiffened. Was Natasha flirting with her? She shook her head as the steel door whined open. These straight girls had a habit of finding their bi-lines when they drank too much. Carmen couldn't fall into that again.

When have I ever? She couldn't remember. It had happened, that was certain. Sometime when she was young, right? She'd fallen into a situation and then—

The door crashed against the toe of Carmen's shoe, derailing her train of thought. She needed to get away from here before something bad happened, be it in a resurfacing memory or in real life.

Except Natasha still had her bag.

"Natasha?" Carmen yanked the door wide open again. "Wait."

The lobby could've eaten Carmen's apartment. It almost reminded her of a fancy Manhattan hotel's lobby, the kind she'd only glimpsed in passing on a walk across Midtown, every surface sleek, the ceiling high, with lounge chairs forming an exclusive circle in one corner. A hum toward the back hinted at a motor, maybe for an elevator. To Carmen's left, a broad staircase ascended to the next floor.

"Natasha?" she called again, hurrying upward.

She should've never let that drunk woman drag her stuff away. Carmen's keys, wallet, subway card, and phone were all inside.

The second floor was quiet. No sounds of wayward footsteps or drunken giggling, only the muffled noise of a sitcom laugh track behind a closed door. Carmen hurried up the next flight of stairs to the top floor.

A brief hallway greeted her with a purple-brown carpet and too-bright bulbs glaring from the ceiling. Five apartments, five doors, four of them shut firm. The one at the end hung slightly ajar, and the sounds of commotion spilled through the narrow gap. Too many people to be Natasha's place.

How do you know? Carmen asked herself. *She could have a bunch of roommates. A big family. They could be having a party of their own.*

She strode up the hall, past the shut doors, to the one at the end. A brass plate reflected gleaming ceiling light, but the actual apartment number had eroded over time, leaving an uncertain carving in the metal. What the hell did Natasha put on her address?

Carmen's lips parted to call for Natasha again, but the noise within grew clearer as her shoes stopped inches from the door. These were not the sounds of a typical apartment get-together. Not even a party as she knew it. No bass line, no hoots and howls of hard drinking or party games.

Light orchestral music seeped through the gap between the door and its frame, and the commotion, even when Carmen couldn't discern individual words, wore the atmosphere of aristocracy. She wouldn't have recognized it without having heard it plenty of times before.

The apartment sounded like the golden masquerade.

Carmen spread her arms to brace her hands on the wall to either side of the doorframe and leaned her ear close to the wood. Could she be hearing it wrong?

She didn't think so. Through the pitching and tossing of unclear conversation, she thought she made out the voices of Camilla, maybe Cassilda, and that strange deep tone of the Stranger.

Carmen withdrew one hand from the wall. Her palm hovered over the wood. It felt cool without even touching her skin. One push, and the golden light would wash over her.

A GAME IN YELLOW

"What are you doing?" a giggling voice asked.

Carmen swirled around and found Natasha leaning from another apartment doorway, her cheek smushed against the frame. Gentle music faded behind her, a song coming to an end.

"Looking for you," Carmen said. "I need my bag."

"Oh. Right."

Natasha pried herself off the doorframe, rubbed the bridge of her nose, and slinked back into her apartment without another word. The door lingered open, waiting.

Carmen waited, too. In the new quiet left by Natasha's faded music, she heard the party again from the unnumbered apartment, so alike to her dreams and reading that she could believe the golden masquerade had bloomed behind her, a yellow flower rising through Astoria concrete into the top floor of this apartment building.

Another song danced in from Natasha's open doorway. A mellow acoustic guitar and subtle bass paved the way for lyrics.

Along the shore the cloud waves break,
The twin suns sink behind the lake.

The song sounded decades old, maybe by the Mamas & the Papas or whichever band did the original "Venus" years before Bananarama's cover. Its singer—she sounded eerily familiar, less like Carmen had heard her on the radio or from her phone, more like someone she'd passed busking on the street.

A discomforting atmosphere swelled through the top floor. Maybe it had always lived here, paying the rent like Natasha and her neighbors. Or maybe it was a new visitor, like Carmen. She wondered if Natasha could've rifled through the bag and skimmed lines from *The King in Yellow* in the time Carmen was searching for the right apartment.

But if so, shouldn't she wander off like Roddy from last night? His reading from the play hadn't affected anyone around him.

Then again, Roddy had only been tipsy at worst. Natasha was sloshed. How should Carmen know if that made Natasha's mind slippery, letting the play slide off her thoughts and into the world? Carmen couldn't say how this worked. Could the play itself become inebriated if read through drunken eyes? It might forget to cling to a single mind, its performance turning sloppy, with the performers making the best of every onstage mishap.

Whether Natasha had read or not, Carmen needed to take the pages away. She left the apartment door at the hall's end and crossed Natasha's threshold.

The place was a disaster. Shredded cardboard littered the linoleum floor at the entrance. A round table bridged the kitchen and living room, its surface buried beneath a mountain of cereal boxes, beer cans, and chip bags. The same decorations littered the kitchen's narrow countertop. Ancient brown-yellow stains dribbled from the freezer down the refrigerator's once-white face. Clothing and towels draped every surface of the living room, and Carmen couldn't tell at a glance what was clean or what was dirty. More cardboard dotted the living room carpet, mixed with food packaging and the contents of a spilled-over ashtray.

"Those are my roommate's," Natasha said, slogging past Carmen. "I wouldn't smoke. All this stuff is hers, actually. You should see my bedroom. It's pristine."

Carmen forced herself to nod. "I knew that."

A guffaw thundered up Natasha's throat and slammed against her pursed lips. Around her, that song went on playing from an unclear source. Carmen gritted her teeth. This was a different beat than she'd heard in her dreams, the lyrics punctuated and then accompanied by 1960s-sounding guitar licks, but the voice—

Strange is the night where black stars rise,
And strange moons circle through the skies.

—it was Cassilda, exactly as she sang in Carmen's dream.

That, or her memory of the dream had changed upon hearing the song. The latter made the most sense, and she desperately needed things to make sense right now.

"Who's this artist?" Carmen asked, spinning a finger as if mimicking a record. "She's so familiar."

"You don't know?" Natasha asked. "You're so funny, Carmen."

She toddled backward into the kitchen and rummaged through the garbage until she found a bag with a few chips left inside.

Carmen stepped away, and her foot crunched on something she hoped wasn't a roach. "Isn't that your roommate's?"

"Don't tattle," Natasha said. "You're supposed to be different from the other office girls."

Carmen flinched, taken aback. "I am. I'm the different one."

"Mm." Natasha stuffed a pair of chips into her mouth. Her nose wrinkled, suggesting the chips were stale, but she was either too hungry or too proud to keep from chewing and swallowing them. "I have to do this. She hates herself. I do too, but for different reasons. That's the secret to the world, Carmen. Every woman hates herself."

Carmen looked down at her clothes as if she were wearing such hatred.

"Christ, you're as clueless as my ex," Natasha said, giggling before stuffing another chip between her lips. "Don't you ever talk to other women?"

Carmen was quiet.

Natasha stopped chewing. "What happened? School friends betrayed you? Someone broke your heart? Or did you break someone else's?"

Aja.

Carmen gritted her teeth. That name again, the one from the office, from the golden masquerade, invading her head with virus-like tenacity.

"My bag," Carmen said, sterner now. "I need it."

Natasha raised her eyebrows in surprise—news to her—and then pointed into the living room with a crumb-dotted finger.

Carmen turned away. The sooner she was out of here, the better. She kicked through the mystery roommate's detritus, past the couch of lumpy towels, and found her bag crumpled against the cream-colored wall. Her knees bent as she squatted to grab it, stand up, and hurry out of here.

But when she stretched again to her feet, her gaze locked on a broad framed photograph clinging to the wall. She hadn't noticed it on approach, her eyes only on her bag.

The photograph captured the breadth of a gorgeous forest from a hilltop.

"My sister took that photo," Natasha said. "She was hiking in the Catskills last fall, a different area than we'll all be going to for work, I think. I loved it so much, she had it blown up for me. It was too pretty to hide in her phone."

"Yeah," Carmen muttered.

A GAME IN YELLOW

She could understand wanting to adorn this trashed apartment tucked into the city's concrete with scenery of gorgeous autumn foliage flourishing in lovely wilderness.

But beauty wasn't what had caught her attention. The leaves were turning later as the cold took longer to arrive each year. A dazzling array of reds, oranges, golds, and browns should have filled the trees and flitted off of them in colorful clouds.

Instead, a summer tinge clutched the foliage. Autumn had only just started when Natasha's sister took this photo, the season kissing the treetops with the beginnings of death and turning the surrounding forest into hills of yellow.

The leaves seemed to dance on their branches, entrancing Carmen to watch. She could imagine figures darting beneath that sickly canopy, a whole world tucked beneath the yellow. Castles hidden in the Catskills, cities among the hills, and masks watching from beneath the foliage, their eyes peering through eyeholes and forest cover and the glass of the photo frame.

Carmen tugged her gaze back to Natasha's living room.

"I have to go," she said, blustering from the wall.

"You're not supposed to," Natasha said, a taunt in her voice.

Carmen closed her eyes and rolled them behind her lids. She'd agreed to take Natasha home, nothing more. Hell, she hadn't even agreed to that—Liza had forced the responsibility onto Carmen, who'd been too stunned to argue.

Natasha spoke again, louder now. "Guess you're not as obedient as your girlfriend thinks."

One shoe clacked on the linoleum at the apartment door as Carmen froze in place. "What did you say?"

She looked over her shoulder and found Natasha looming close by. Her steps hadn't made the floor garbage crunch and rustle like Carmen's had, and she didn't look so drunk as before either. Same as Blanca last night. Carmen seemed a poor judge of telling when someone was hammered.

"Your girlfriend," Natasha said. "She told me you were a good sport. A good pet."

Songs that the Hyades shall sing,
Where flap the tatters of the King.

Music went on guitaring around Carmen. How long was this song? And how long would she have to stand here, calculating Natasha's words?

Pet. How could she know that nickname applied to Carmen? Blanca wouldn't have arranged for Carmen to meet a third without telling her. She'd been diligent in introducing Smoke.

But then, hadn't the same happened with Natasha?

"She . . . wanted me here?" Carmen asked. "With you?"

Natasha leered, a wanting ache in her dark eyes. "Did you really think our run-in outside Rico's was a coincidence?"

Carmen softened all the way down to her bones. Blanca had played the same game as she'd tried with Smoke, situating a meetup last night, extenuating circumstances tonight, spreading the gameboard to play with Carmen. Smoke had been plan A last night, but Blanca had already plotted out a contingency—Natasha. Yet another woman to share the load of an increasingly difficult girlfriend.

Am I really that much trouble for her? Carmen wondered.

Natasha stepped closer, her foot maneuvering between mounds of trash. "We've worked together for a long time, and I know most of the people in our little territory, but you're the quiet one. The unknown in my space." Her hand slid onto Carmen's cheek, palm cold against her skin. "I want to meet the stranger, and now I have a chance to find out what makes you so strange."

Carmen let her bag shift from shoulder to arm. "I have to get in the mood."

She squatted down amid the apartment refuse, planted her bag between her knees, and began to rummage through its innards. There wasn't much inside. Her fingers brushed the flat face of a yellowy paper.

Natasha stepped sideways, planting herself behind Carmen. "What's in there? Drugs?"

"Better," Carmen said.

Her fingers found the paper's edges, and its sibling pages, and she drew out what she had of *The King in Yellow*. It might have grown since leaving the office.

Someone would read it tonight. Natasha leaned over Carmen's shoulder, her skin radiating warm curiosity. Her jacket stroked Carmen's neck.

Should she be allowed to read? Carmen couldn't say. She had no idea what would happen if two people read from the play at the same time.

But Natasha's skin was not the only radiant surface. The pages shimmered at the bottom of Carmen's sight, as if the play had been inked on gold foil or on a pressing of autumn-kissed yellow leaves from Natasha's wall photo. Natasha couldn't get Carmen in the mood, but the play knew her. It was a convincing lover in its own way, the anticipation of survivor's euphoria shooting a sallow-yet-welcome thrill into her body.

Carmen's heartbeat rocked up her arm and through her hand. The pages pounded.

The walls pounded.

Her clit pounded.

The song pounded.

Song of my soul, my voice is dead,
Die thou, unsung, as tears unshed
Shall dry and die in
Lost Carcosa.

And that eternal song seemed to fade at last as Carmen once again read from the play, picking up with what she'd last glimpsed:

CAMILLA	You, sir, should unmask.
STRANGER	Indeed?
CASSILDA	Indeed it's time. We have all laid aside disguise but you.
STRANGER	I wear no m—

A stillness holds THE STRANGER.

CAMILLA	(impatient) Mask. The word is mask.
STRANGER	We are no longer as we should be.
CASSILDA	I don't understand.
CAMILLA	Nor do I.
STRANGER	One has come who does not belong. There is another. There is a Natasha.

The Act becomes unclear. The part becomes unclear. There is only the golden masquerade, and the scandal, and a sense of death in the air so pervasive that even an observer can feel it and thank the heavens they are not part of this nightmare incarnate.

A GAME IN YELLOW

CAMILLA   Her name is *what*?
CASSILDA   Natasha.
CAMILLA   Surely you mean *Catasha*? Or even *Canatasha*?
CASSILDA   No, my love. He said Natasha.

Enter NATASHA. She wears no splendor over her body, only a shimmering suggestion of garment that forces the air around her to waver and shift. No solid mask adorns her face, only this same obfuscating distortion. The effect reminds CARMEN of television static back when that was a thing. Signals have come undone between the golden masquerade and her mind.

NATASHA   Carmen? Is that you?
CAMILLA   (drawing Carmen aside) Don't speak to it. And don't let it speak to you.
CARMEN   But I don't understand. I know her. Don't I?
CAMILLA   You don't. You *can't*. She hasn't the decency to at least guise herself in the right namesake.

The music of the golden masquerade grows harrowed and frantic. Harsh light flares from the balcony overlooking the Lake of Hali, as if the sky is about to explode. Something is wrong. Everything is wrong. Amid the swelling yellow atmosphere, only THE STRANGER is distinct.

STRANGER   What dread invitation brought this one to this golden place?

| CAMILLA | We must forget her. |
| CASSILDA | We will forget all. |

THE STRANGER extends an arm to one side, opening his cloak and forming a curtain of yellow behind the unsettled distortion of NATASHA.

| STRANGER | You wished to meet the stranger tonight, and now you have. But I am not gentle. |

THE STRANGER begins to fold his cloak around NATASHA. She peers over one shoulder, her expression unclear through the effect she has on the air itself. She might be serene. She might be frightened out of her mind. Has there been no prior warning of madness? There is no solid form beneath the cloak of THE STRANGER, only a twisting jaundiced shadow.

| CARMEN | Wait. You're the Stranger. Your name isn't right either. |
| STRANGER | My name has every right. The wrong is in me. And this wrong joins me thus. |

THE STRANGER finishes folding his cloak around himself again, but there is no misshapenness to suggest there's anyone underneath. Not NATASHA.

Not even THE STRANGER himself.

16

An Intimation of Doom

A HAND OF FABRIC COATED Carmen's face as she gasped to sitting up straight. To leaning against a wall, her trembling hand diving past her waistline and rubbing with a slick fury against the marshy softness between her legs.

She opened her mouth, uncertain whether to protest or cry out in glee. A place of yellowness and ruin glowed behind her eyelids, beneath the smothering fabric, restrictive as a plastic bag, stealing her breath into a muffled sigh. The dullness of life had faded again into streaking sweat and rippling fire. She had forgotten how good the play could make her feel.

Maybe that made her troublesome. Too demanding. No wonder Blanca looked scared sometimes when Carmen craved such abuse. And no wonder Carmen loved the pages of *The King in Yellow*, rising bidden or unbidden into her mind, inhuman and therefore beyond reproach. Unliving and therefore eternal. The perfect abuser. Or lover.

Yes, she thought. *Smother me.*

She couldn't breathe, and that only stoked the fire beneath her skin to lick with greater ferocity, the tongues of flames ravenous in meeting her fingers until her lungs ached, her nerves blazed. This had been her desire from the start. If only she'd known how much she'd truly wanted Blanca to take her breath away.

Blanca.

Her softness. Her beauty. Carmen's breath surged beneath the fabric, her fingers quaking, everything inside her swelling to a tempestuous surge she couldn't keep locked inside.

"Blanca!" she screamed. And came.

Only in the shallow breaths of new clarity did she remember what she'd read from *The King in Yellow*. Something impossible. Herself, in the play. And someone else, too.

Carmen dragged the fabric off her face and held it out to see better. It was Natasha's jacket.

"Nat"—Carmen swallowed, still gasping—"asha?"

No one leaned over Carmen's shoulder. The garbage lingered across the apartment, but it offered no sign of Natasha. There was only the sickening sense that what Carmen had taken for cream-colored walls were yellower than she'd observed, their cream having spoiled while she read her pages.

Something thumped in the hallway. Maybe Natasha had locked herself out?

Carmen wiped her hand on Natasha's jacket, stuffed her pages into her bag, and pried herself off the floor. Everything ached, as if she'd been restrained for some length of time. That hadn't happened, though. *Nothing* had happened. She gripped the doorknob and yanked the apartment door open.

No one stood in the hallway. Carmen peered out, glanced down the way—still no one—and then to the hall's dead end.

The brass plate was no longer scarred with its odd symbol. It now read 35. An ordinary apartment number for what was likely an ordinary apartment, solidly part of this building. It might always have been ordinary.

Or it might have been a sickly claw snatching Natasha away and then hiding its hand as if it had done nothing wrong.

Stop it, Carmen thought. *There was nothing in there because there's no such thing as the golden masquerade. Say it.*

Her tongue slid between her teeth, but she didn't make a sound.

Say it. There's no such thing as Hastur. No such thing as Alar. As Carcosa. Say it. Pretend Blanca's ordering you. Say. It. Any of it.

Carmen opened her mouth at a whisper. "There's no such thing as Natasha."

She slapped her palm flush against her lips, but it wasn't like she could snatch the words out of the air. They were said. They could not be unsaid.

"No, no, no."

Carmen plunged her hand into her bag again and dug up the pages. They creased between her fingers into something of a sideways facial expression.

"You didn't," Carmen snapped. "You didn't!"

She started to leaf through the pages, hoping to catch Natasha's name. Maybe there was a part where she came back in Act II.

Except that didn't make any sense. The play couldn't wipe

someone out of this world, and it couldn't take them. There was nowhere for them to go. Worse, to read would drown Carmen in another moment of sexual reverie. She didn't react to the play like Roddy, maybe like anyone else. Maybe that meant she could do something about it.

"I can fix this." Carmen shook the pages, flapping in her hand. "You have to fix this."

But how? She was a fuck-up in every way. Nothing special. Even her reaction to the play might have only been a matter of immersive protection, like building up a tolerance to a drug. Smoke had fed it to her by sentence, by paragraph, before Carmen dove headfirst into these pages. Until they'd absorbed her into their own world, full of character and menace.

What about Blanca, then? She wasn't a fuck-up at all. With her smarts, capacity for planning, sense of control that she didn't have to defer to others, couldn't she fix this?

Except Carmen couldn't tell her. The explanation wouldn't make sense, and if it did—why would Blanca stay? Instead of a solution, Carmen would have an absence. An ending.

If I can't tell Blanca, then what would Blanca do?

She wouldn't have landed herself in this position in the first place. And soon, she would get rid of Carmen and never risk finding herself at the whim of a fuck-up now beholden to a play with a mind of its own.

"You can't do this to me!" Carmen shrieked, shaking the pages again. "Fix it, you son of a bitch!"

Steel hinges squealed, and Carmen wheeled from Natasha's doorway to face the end of the hall. Apartment 35's door had creaked open, and an elderly man peered through the crack.

A GAME IN YELLOW

Liver spots tracked across his bald head like a small animal's footprints in the snow. One eye was near squinted shut, while the other glared with blue disdain.

"What you scream for?" he asked, his accent thick, maybe Russian. "Too late for screaming."

Carmen slinked back from Natasha's door, clutching her bag to her chest. The pages rumpled against its side as if protesting.

"You don't live here?" The man chinned toward Carmen, the stairs. "Go, or I give something to scream for. You go now."

She thought he might shut his door, but he waited, watching her retreat toward the stairs. He needed to see her gone. Why wouldn't he? The play was ink on paper. She must've looked out of her mind, chastising its pages, believing they could mix parts of her into their already-written words and drink people like Natasha out of the world.

Except the play was not only ink on paper. She couldn't lie to herself well enough to pretend its mundanity. Smoke would've had no reason to show it to her otherwise.

Smoke—the realization hit Carmen as she hurried down the flights of steps, aiming to hurry out of this building before anyone else caught sight of her. Back to the train platform. Back to home.

Natasha had run into Carmen outside Rico's last night. Maybe she'd been telling the truth about it being no coincidence, maybe not. She'd known that nickname—*Pet*.

But which woman had she heard it from? Carmen had been with Blanca, yes, but also Smoke. Did Natasha know which was Carmen's girlfriend? Carmen had entertained Natasha's advances thinking they were part of Blanca's commands, but for all she knew, Smoke had been the one to approach Natasha, tell her about Carmen's particularities, and arrange whatever the hell tonight was going to be before *The King in Yellow* set to work. Smoke might have been behind everything.

But why?

17

That Dismal Place

THE APARTMENT STAIRWELL WAS DARK and ringing with muffled voices when Carmen stepped inside. One of the ceiling lights had gone out, and the others kept winking as if they'd made a sly comment that Carmen couldn't understand. She didn't care about the lightbulbs or the yellow sheen she imagined upon the walls.

Only those voices. Some of them were neighbors, their soundtrack the nature of apartment living. But she knew the others better, growing clearer as she neared her apartment door.

"—kind of patience—nothing to prove—"

That was Blanca. Annoyance coiled in her tone, measured as always to the exact amount she wanted her listener to feel. Carmen half hoped she was on the phone, but that seemed unlikely.

Especially when Smoke answered.

"I mean it, B." She sounded upset, nothing like the cool disaffection Carmen had known these past couple of weeks. "It's not anything I would've said if I didn't have good reason. I'm sorry, I shouldn't have suggested it."

"Yeah," Blanca said. "I don't put up with shit. You know this."

"You put up with hers," Smoke said, and gave a pained laugh. "Must be a relief, letting someone else take over, never having to worry if she's pushed too far. Even when she does."

"That's none of your business."

A sudden quiet seized the hall as Carmen reached the door, stealing away Blanca's and Smoke's voices, as well as the sounds from every neighboring apartment.

Smoke's next words came in Spanish. They were halting sentences, the cadence of a second language she wasn't used to anymore. Blanca's replies hit with rapid fluency, and the two of them went back and forth, never heated, but with a firm severity between them.

Carmen doubted she could have followed even if she'd learned more than a handful of Spanish, her mind a species of wrinkled slug that Blanca had miraculously come to adore.

But for how much longer? They had to be talking about her again.

If either of them happened to open the apartment door now, they'd find her standing here. Listening.

She tiptoed back to the stairwell and sneaked down the steps. An apartment door opened, and she didn't have to look to know it was hers. She ducked beneath the stairs, waiting in the shadows.

Smoke swept down the steps. Carmen spotted her only

A GAME IN YELLOW

briefly—wiping her eyes, leaving mascara trails on her cheeks and the back of her hand—and then she was out the door, gone into the night.

What the fuck had happened up there? Carmen couldn't imagine Blanca having the urge to drive anyone to tears, or that Smoke had enough heart to have her feelings hurt. Maybe Blanca had changed her mind about subletting the playroom. Or maybe Smoke had given too much of herself to Blanca when Blanca had only wanted a temporary third after all. Someone to bear a little of Carmen's demands. With that having failed last night, maybe they'd seen the last of Smoke.

Except that couldn't be true. Some of her remained in Carmen's bag, incarnated into yellow pages.

Carmen whispered under her breath as the outside door slammed shut: "There's no such thing as Smoke."

She could almost imagine the disappearance right there on the street, with Smoke puffing into a cloud of her namesake to be blown away by the September wind.

But Carmen could also imagine Smoke lingering. Choking the world. Standing outside the apartment building in stubborn refusal to give up, sucking her damn vape while wiping her face dry. Regaining her confidence. Ready to storm back inside and try for Blanca again.

Carmen shook her head, retreating. Her mind wasn't a wrinkled slug; it was a hollow in her skull. What, did she truly believe she could pull a reverse-Tinkerbell *clap if you believe in fairies* against Smoke and poof her out of existence? Natasha wasn't gone over anything Carmen had done.

It was the play. And Smoke was too cunning to let it vanish her off the face of the earth.

Carmen stomped up the stairs, purposely noisy. She wanted Blanca to have warning that she wouldn't be alone. And if Smoke came back, she would find them together. The way they belonged.

"Sorry I'm late," Carmen said, shoving the apartment door open.

Blanca sat stone-faced on the couch. A fire rumbled inside her, but it wasn't the euphoric lust Carmen had burned with earlier in Natasha's apartment. This was cold fire, cold rage. Something Carmen didn't want to touch.

But she could almost miss it, too. Blanca was a statue, wielding such immense control of expression that Carmen could've believed Blanca was only tired. Could almost ignore the indignation radiating off her skin and filling the apartment.

She flashed Carmen a tired smile. "I missed you."

"You, too," Carmen said, dropping her bag by the door. "Was that Smoke I saw heading out?"

"Maybe," Blanca said, and her smile died. "She needed correcting about something. We sorted it out. She'll come back when she's feeling better."

What exactly had Smoke suggested? Blanca leaving Carmen for Smoke? Living together? Were they already sleeping together without Carmen? She'd given her blessing the other night, so why not take it for granted?

It didn't sound like Blanca. For one, she was too good to do that. And even if she weren't, she maintained control with near-dogmatic zeal, and she couldn't control a situation where two people knew a secret. Too easy for the other person to slip. A shared secret would turn Blanca inside out with stress.

A GAME IN YELLOW

All the more reason to believe Smoke was behind that mess with Natasha. Carmen needed to set herself straight.

She slid from her shoes and strode toward the couch. "And how about you? How're you doing?"

One hand cupped Blanca's cheek, another stroked her hair, and Carmen kissed Blanca's forehead. Then her temple. Her cheek. Her lips, soft as a landing butterfly.

Blanca sighed hard as she shook herself loose. "I'm a mess right now."

Carmen looked her over—pajamas, robe, hair gone wild—and shook her head. "When you're a mess is when I want to kiss you most."

"You're a mess, too," Blanca said.

Carmen hoped to hear a Natasha-like giggle after that, a batting of eyelashes maybe, and then remembered those were un-Blanca traits. She was more likely to smirk, devising a scenario and her next ten steps behind her eyes.

But there was no smirk. No sly look. As usual, Blanca could see right through Carmen's attraction and into her earnest desperation, and why should Blanca want to be the sponge who cleaned up Carmen's latest disaster?

"Isn't this what we wanted?" Carmen asked. "For me to get better?"

"This isn't better. What happened to you?" Blanca looked Carmen up and down. "I'm starting to think you need a doctor. Or a therapist."

"They can't help me with this." Carmen lowered her hands to Blanca's sides and laid them on her hips. "Only you can."

"Do you want help with whatever this is?" Blanca asked.

"You've been so checked out. I was still hoping getting away from the city next week would help get your head back to the world, but I don't know what's with you anymore. Starting to think you like it."

"It doesn't care what I like," Carmen said.

Her teeth clenched against her will, as if an unseen hand puppeted her mouth from the inside and no longer wanted her to speak. She wasn't certain where those words had come from or what they meant. Not entirely, at least.

Blanca ran a hand down from her eyes to her chin, muttering Spanish under her palm.

"I'm sorry," Carmen said, wrapping her arms around Blanca's shoulders.

Blanca let her, but she didn't hug back. That didn't seem right. Had Smoke made her too angry for affection? Did she not love Carmen anymore?

No, that wasn't it. Blanca's coldness came as part of the game, her measured nature turning to calculations and sexual opportunity. Carmen understood that—being taken by the game was exactly what she needed. Punishment would cement her as Blanca's girlfriend. As her *Pet*. No one else's.

Carmen let her arms slide down Blanca's, her hands again feeling at Blanca's sides.

"Carmen." Blanca sounded annoyed.

"It'll be fine," Carmen said. "Everything will be fine. You have just the right idea. You take control."

"You don't know what you're saying. When do you ever know?" Blanca shoved Carmen's hands away. "I'm not in the mood right now."

"It doesn't have to be sex. Just take control. Call me Pet."

A GAME IN YELLOW

"Carmen."

"I'm yours. What you heard before was wrong. You can have happiness. I can make you whole."

Blanca broke from Carmen's touch, from the couch, and stumbled toward the bedroom, a wild, fearful look twisting her features.

Carmen froze in place, her hands still cupping the space where Blanca had been sitting. She stared past the back of the couch, to that gentle form in the dark, and realized the condition of the night. Of course Blanca couldn't try controlling Carmen right now. She needed every ounce of willpower to keep from crying.

"You don't have to hold back," Carmen said, rising from the cushions. "It's okay to cry."

Blanca blinked at her. "You don't know what I need to do. You don't know anything."

"Fine, yes, I'm a mess." Carmen felt tears coming, too, but she wouldn't hide them. "What's the alternative to messiness? Trying to control everything, keeping it perfectly measured, forever? What kind of life is that?"

"Carmen." Blanca paused, teeth setting behind her lips.

"See?" Carmen asked, harsher than she wanted. "You're doing it now. You can't even fly off the handle. Everything has to be just right."

Blanca's eyes had turned glassy, and there was a coldness in them Carmen recognized, but she didn't have Blanca's innate perception. Was it rage? Hurt? Despair? Mania? Some confused kind of joy? She couldn't know unless Blanca let it spill out in a messy tempest. If the game had to end for her to release this control, so be it.

And if *they* had to end, too?

Carmen softened, hurrying around the couch to Blanca's front. "I'm sorry, I'm sorry, this wasn't fair. I was wrong. It's only—I didn't just see Smoke leave. I heard you get mad at her, like a bare-faced, true kind of angry. Like you could be more honest with her than with me."

"Honest?" Blanca asked.

"More open," Carmen said. "More yourself. Can't you do that with me, too?"

Blanca slipped closer, her breath hot on Carmen's face. "I've never been anything with you I didn't want to be. If you want something else, find it. Be it. Take control of your life."

They held in place for a long moment. Carmen almost felt like Blanca might kiss her after all, their aggravation sparking the passion she'd been searching for tonight.

But Blanca only inhaled shakily, fighting back a cry, and then headed into the bedroom. The door clicked shut behind her. Carmen wasn't even worth a slam.

"I wasn't in the mood, either," she whispered. "Everything's okay."

She wished she could know that for certain. Everything had spiraled out of control tonight from the moment Liza had foisted Natasha into Carmen's responsibility. She'd never wanted that. Control was never anything she'd dreamed about, at least that she knew.

But what did she know to be true anymore? There was herself, and there was *The King in Yellow*, a trawler across her murky mind. It had rescued thrills she hadn't meant to let slip beneath those waters, but it had also dredged up miseries she'd meant to let drown and be forgotten. Inadequacies, uncertainties, even trauma.

And Blanca was suffering the weight.

Take control of your life.

Carmen took a step toward the bedroom, faltered, and crumpled against the wall outside the playroom. In demanding Blanca let go of her control, Carmen might have found exactly that. Not because Blanca was choosing it. More that Carmen had a profound sense she was eroding Blanca's will. That she would be left broken in the end by Carmen's hand.

Same as someone else. A name that kept unspooling rope-like from Carmen's head, and same as Blanca, it refused to tie Carmen down and keep her. She would keep running from her life. From that name.

Aja.

18

The Yellow Sign

As CAMILLA and CASSILDA join the dance, CAMILLA leading and CASSILDA following, CARMEN walks arm in arm with THE STRANGER at the masquerade's center. They are neither exiting the stage via the staircase nor approaching the balcony, only stepping without progress as if the masquerade revolves around them.

CARMEN	You take me upon the dance floor, but you have not begun to lead.
STRANGER	I do not dance.
CARMEN	Will you talk with me, then?
STRANGER	I speak only what must be said.
CARMEN	You believe you're more attractive when mysterious. What do you do then?
STRANGER	Of late, I take after you. I become a

	player, of stage and of games. I set my mark and move my piece.
CARMEN	As in chess?
STRANGER	A chess of shadows, the pieces lost and dim, lengthening as if standing within Carcosa.
CARMEN	You aren't afraid to speak its name.
STRANGER	I neither fear the setting of black suns from amber skies nor dark shadows upon a golden masquerade. Here, I play my piece. It bears the shape that is truth incarnate.

THE STRANGER raises a pale hand gone sallow in the chandelier light. A symbol slices across the flesh of his palm and curls to either side, set by burned ink. It resembles a mark cut into a brass plate on an apartment door.

STRANGER	Mark you, the Yellow Sign.

―

The morning peered into the playroom like a Peeping Tom expecting the sapphic art to come to erotic life across the walls. The mermaid print lay on the floor again, its glass shattered from its frame.

Carmen found herself kneeling naked in front of the playroom wall, its stab wounds again unveiled. Had she slept in here after the squabble with Blanca last night? She couldn't be sure. She didn't remember sleeping.

And she didn't remember seeing the white rope Blanca had

A GAME IN YELLOW

used to bind her last time they'd played with Smoke. It looked to have gone dingy with years and turned a sickly yellow.

Where it now twined around Carmen's forearms.

Both hands were going blue, and they aimed upward and ahead as if she were praying to the black holes in the wall. Straining only made the ropes bite harder into her flesh.

"Dimetrodon," Carmen whispered. "Dimetrodon, dimetrodon." She snapped her fingers and then thrashed forward, but the knots held tight. "Blanca? Sweetie, help me?"

No answer.

Just take control, Carmen had said. She could only hope it was Blanca who'd listened, and not someone else. And now, who was here to listen? Blanca had a café shift today and might have headed out early to find a cure for a wounded heart. No one would be home until this afternoon.

Must be a relief.

Smoke's words. As if this surprise morning bondage might be Smoke's desire.

That story about finding *The King in Yellow* in Mexico swept a desert wind through Carmen's thoughts. Smoke had told it practically unprompted, hadn't she? An answer to an unasked question.

It had been important to her that Carmen and Blanca know that answer, to have an idea of Smoke's past doings and whereabouts. Was there something else underneath that Smoke didn't want them to know? Didn't want them to go looking for?

What did she really have to do with that play?

Must be a relief, letting someone else take over. Smoke had insinuated she meant Blanca, but the same could apply to Carmen's arms right now.

Or it could mean other pieces of her, bound by *The King in Yellow*.

"You can't have me," Carmen snapped. "I'm not Natasha. I belong to Blanca." She thought again of Smoke. "And you can't have Blanca. She's mine."

After a few minutes of twisting her arms and chewing at the knots, Carmen wrestled to standing and stumbled to the kitchen, where a steak knife severed the knot at her wrists. Once one stretch of rope slithered away, the rest followed.

But they left a pattern in their wake, across the undersides of Carmen's forearms, one she recognized. It had come to her in a dream. And before that, in the marking on a brass plate in Natasha's apartment building.

The Yellow Sign.

~

Another late run to work, but Carmen made sure to stop at the deli this time. Liza's capacity to forgive had no limits so long as someone refilled it now and then with an egg sandwich bribe. Carmen hurried out a quick text while in line.

CARMEN: Egg day!

LIZA: thanks

The messages appeared as lavender and yellow blobs on either side of Carmen's phone screen, but she imagined a transcription of them would echo an old internet chatroom.

Or a playscript.

No, no more of *The King in Yellow* today. She had to steer her focus to anything else, like the weird looks she was getting as she paid for the bagel box and egg sandwich, or the stares she caught at the Queensboro station, or the man who grinned at her on the corner and said something lost to the cacophony of traffic.

She checked her face in her phone camera outside the office building lobby, pretending she was taking a selfie—nothing looked off. In fact, better than usual. No bags haunted her eyes, no redness surrounding her irises.

More a mask of the ideal Carmen than the real thing.

―~―

"Bagels."

Carmen made the announcement and then placed them in the breakroom without taking one for herself. Her fingers wandered her keyboard and mouse, clocking her in to work, but she didn't start with any data-entry log.

She instead popped open the search database and typed in a single word: Smoke.

Nothing popped up. Not even a middle name or an alias. It had been a long shot, being a common word, but that was all she had to work with. Smoke had never divulged whether that was a legal name or a nickname, whether she'd changed it from something else. Carmen couldn't guess Smoke's address, whether she had her own place, if she lived with roommates or couch-surfed with friends. Was she even a New York resident on paper?

Every part of her was an enigma, given shape only by her words, as if she'd seeped out of nothingness. No more real than a character in a play.

Where there was Smoke, there had to be fire, but Carmen couldn't seem to locate it.

Who did you invite into our lives? Carmen wondered, and then felt immediate guilt. Blanca might've met Smoke while bartending, but she'd only bound herself and Carmen tighter against that mysterious woman for Carmen's sake. Without her need, Smoke might have been a brief presence, never ingratiating herself into their love life. Never showing them *The King in Yellow*.

A sudden knocking shot Carmen from her seat with a gasp. She could have coughed up her beating heart.

"Whoa, didn't mean to scare you," Liza said, peering over the cubicle wall. "Get home all right last night?"

"Sure." Carmen swallowed hard. "Here, I forgot to bring you this."

She locked her fingers around Liza's foil-wrapped egg sandwich and raised it up the cubicle wall, an animal offering her food to a zookeeper.

Liza accepted it, but she didn't smile or crack a joke. Her gaze studied the cubicle's inside, not the dormant computer or Carmen's tote bag, but Carmen herself.

Why the scrutiny? Had she done something? Bought the wrong kind of sandwich?

Moments of stillness and quiet passed between her and Liza before Carmen realized she was the last person to see Natasha yesterday. And if what Carmen thought had happened in that apartment last night turned out to be true, she was the last to see Natasha alive at all. Liza had sent them off together—multiple people would've noticed, even while tipsy. And that elderly neighbor with the mean blue eye had seen Carmen out.

What did that picture look like once pieced together?

Carmen found her mouth dry. She licked her lips. "Did Natasha come in today?"

A GAME IN YELLOW

Liza studied her for another silent moment and then retreated from the cubicle. "I need to see you in my office. Right away."

Carmen listened to her fading footsteps across the thin office carpet. She then grabbed her letter opener and plunged it through her mousepad, carving out another round hole not far from the first. Was that what Liza thought might've happened to Natasha? Why the office meeting? She should call the cops, see if they could stop playing games on their phones in the subway long enough to come up here and arrest Carmen for—what? Death by cursed play? Even if that were true, none of them would believe it. And even if they did, Smoke had probably been the one to set that up, pretending she was Carmen's girlfriend.

At least, Carmen hoped. Maybe it was Blanca. She couldn't ask around without implicating herself.

She pulled the letter opener loose from the mousepad and clacked it against the desk. She then plucked up the mousepad, now with two holes perforating its foamy surface, one at a diagonal tilt from the other, much like the holes in the playroom wall.

Another mask.

No mask. No mask!

Carmen stuffed the mousepad into the garbage. She would get a new one from the supply closet after talking with Liza, supposing she still worked here. Her legs stretched uneasily from her seat. She didn't want to leave her bag unguarded with the play inside after last night, but taking it along to Liza's office would look bizarre. Her hand patted it as if telling it to stay.

As the cubicles slid by, she couldn't remember where Natasha had worked. Which of these little boxes lay decorated with pieces of Natasha's personality? Carmen hadn't gotten to know Natasha well last night, but there was clearly more to her than the amorphous hivemind she'd pretended to be part of here in the office.

There's no such thing as Natasha. Carmen would have to hope the rest of the world had decided that was true.

She hurried on toward Liza's office, passing her coworkers as they returned to their desks with half bagels, quarter bagels, the tiniest dollops of cream cheese they would allow themselves. All of them in masks, only not the kind Carmen thought of when reading and dreaming.

What would they do if they met the Stranger? Would they find him cute in his mysterious nature, or would they ridicule each other for approaching him?

And what mask did Carmen wear when she dreamed herself into the play's world? Something more convincing than Natasha's. Carmen could have found a mirror in that place, but she didn't seem to care while attending the masquerade. Dream Carmen didn't even talk like herself. Real-life disconnection had reflected into a dream disconnection, and the play might have bound her to a vulnerability she couldn't have anticipated.

A slamming door snapped her out of distracted thoughts. She was in Liza's office. Right, that was where she'd been going.

The white-walled room was larger than a cubicle, but not by much. The backs of desktop photo frames stared black rectangles into Carmen, and she forced herself not to think of stab wounds and dark stars.

A GAME IN YELLOW

"Listen, I've overlooked your tardiness before," Liza said, sitting behind her desk and crossing her arms over her white blouse. She did not invite Carmen to sit, but she shook her egg sandwich to catch Carmen's attention. "I appreciate these, and I can keep overlooking it, but not when you force me to see the reason you're late."

How did this have anything to do with Natasha? Carmen blinked hard. The room looked fuzzy. Almost yellow. The suffocating strain of plastic haunted her lips and skin, as if she were only imagining this worktime hassle from within Blanca's sure grasp.

"What reason?" Carmen asked.

Liza aimed the foil to one side and then the other. "Those marks on your arms."

Carmen stuck her arms out in front of her. She was wearing a short-sleeved button-up, the nearest top she could grab this morning. Long sleeves would've served her better, both for the cold office and to hide what Liza, and likely others, had noticed.

Ligature marks patterned Carmen's forearms like snakes dressing her skin. The undersides of her forearms still bore the Yellow Sign with fresh clarity.

"What you do in your private life is your business," Liza went on. "But—"

Carmen cut in. "It's not a customer-facing job."

Liza raised an eyebrow. "Excuse you. We talked about appropriate office demeanor."

"I don't meet our clients," Carmen said. "No one ever sees us except each other. I did nothing wrong. Like you said, what I do in my private life is my business."

"But it's more than that when you bring it to work," Liza said. "Where I have to see it."

Carmen lowered her arms, obscuring Liza's view. "That isn't the problem. Seeing it. Your problem is seeing it makes you think about it."

"More than I'd like."

"And how's that my responsibility?" Carmen neared the desk. "That's your mind, your problem. I'm not telling you what to think. You don't have any idea what it's like to have someone telling you what to do."

Liza raised an open palm. "I don't want to."

"Then why do you think about it?" Carmen asked. "If a woman loves being restrained by another consenting adult, you have a problem with it? Or does it bother you that you don't have as big a problem with it as you'd like? Come on, Liza. You've never enjoyed it when your husband held you down?"

"Carmen, that's exactly what I mean by inappropriate work talk," Liza said. "And it's very unprofessional to bring up my private life."

"After bringing up mine?" Carmen tensed her arms, re-shaping the rope marks. "No, fuck that. I have someone at home. And another woman, too. And besides those two—do you know how exhausting it gets to answer to three voices already? I don't want the goddamn responsibility of where your thoughts go, too."

"Carmen!" Liza's fist crushed the egg sandwich, spurting melted cheese through a crease in the foil. "Go back to your desk and work while I figure out what to do with you."

Her rage simmered in the air. Carmen would not take

A GAME IN YELLOW

responsibility for that, either. She drifted out of Liza's office on apathetic limbs, ready to collapse.

The main office floor was quiet except at one cubicle, where three of her coworkers gathered, giggling over another's phone. Probably a celebrity's change of weight, or hair, or skin. Someone else to judge and then blame for their appearance intruding into onlookers' lives. A target on which the office collective could project every terror and insecurity.

Carmen slid Liza's door shut with a stone in her gut. These poor women. What was their truth? What did they want in the secret place beneath loathing themselves and each other?

They bowed to a dominant influence, same as Carmen, only they didn't realize it. Worse, they weren't getting any fun or love out of it, too busy despising themselves while terrified they might feel like Carmen, act like Smoke, look like Blanca. They cowered from their unique beauty, surrendering to the bodiless tyrannical forces of this world.

But they didn't have to. So Liza wanted Carmen to take responsibility for others' thoughts? Fine. If her coworkers weren't capable of making that decision, Carmen could help them, one submissive to another. She glanced down at the markings on her arms.

It bears the shape that is truth incarnate.

Another world awaited beyond her coworkers' collective self-hatred. And in that world, they might find empowerment. Right now, they submitted to abuse, but they could take control beneath a new influence, the way Carmen had. The submissive set the boundaries.

"Replace one influence with another," she whispered. "Out with the old, and long live the king."

At her desk, she reached into her tote bag and rifled through *The King in Yellow*. The effect would be strongest if she gave her coworkers everything, but she doubted they would read through the flaying stage of Act I. She instead plucked out everything she had of Act II. The plan did not take long to come together.

Cheesy junk goes straight to my hips.
I look fat enough already.
Wish I could eat like you.

And most recent, and most important, Natasha's words: *Every woman hates herself.*

Carmen carried the pages to the copy room, where the copy machine radiated with monstrous heat. It had never been her friend. Never been anyone's friend. She was risking her only tie with Act II outside of Smoke's book.

But for once, the copier took the pages without chewing them into wrinkled chaos. Another sign, more inky than yellow. After some ticking and whirring, a copy of these few Act II pages slid onto the output bay.

Carmen plucked them up. Before making another couple of copies, placing them in the breakroom and at her desk, and heading home for the day, she grabbed a black marker and scribbled another two words beside Act II—Scene 1 at the top of the first page.

The words that would ensure her coworkers read with intent.

Carmen's Diet.

19

Irresistible Truth

THE STRANGER turns another page. An expectation for revelation surrounds him, but he is not interested in reading by request. He will read, but not what is wanted. There are screams here that have been buried. The turn of a page will unearth them.

STRANGER		Act II—Scene 2. Carmen has forgotten the name of the girl, as she has tried to forget all things from this time. In her failure to accomplish this, she has placed a mask of Blanca over the girl's face, years too early for this moment, this night. So guarded is this truth that Carmen will not be read to. She will only suffer a demonstration, as in dreams. As in nightmares.

The stage of stairways falls dark again and then fades into a stormy night and a slick strip of pavement. A car rolls onto this lot and parks at a motel, its frame trembling as if chilled by the rain.

Enter CARMEN as a senior in high school. Her posture, at first emergence from the passenger seat of the car, is weighed by a profound unspoken sadness. She buries it the instant she hears the driver's door open and sees the figure arise with her into the storm.

Enter AJA. She is pretty and dark and brave, and CARMEN is smitten with her. The precipitation chokes her long hair, but it cannot hide her smile in the motel's outer light. She leads CARMEN in a giddy race from the car to the front desk and then out again. A downpour roars around them and yet fails to drown them out. AJA cups her hands around her mouth.

> AJA   (as if to the audience) What did she say to her mother, ladies and gentlemen?
>
> CARMEN   Fuck you!

They charge up the outdoor steps to the second floor, sneakers clanging, voices chanting in fury.

> AJA   What did she say?

A GAME IN YELLOW

CARMEN   Fuck you!
AJA   I can't hear yooou.
CARMEN   Fuck. YOU!

It is a short distance from the top of the stairs to their motel room. AJA struggles with the lock, shaking with raw nerves and long-restrained determination. They are sopping wet by the time they enter the room, but they are young, and careless, and nothing matters, and everything matters.

CARMEN   I want to—
AJA   Yes.

These days, CARMEN speaks her mind, believing she is right to do so. It is not until later that she decides she is mistaken, becoming the quiet CARMEN who meets BLANCA in the city. On this night, CARMEN and AJA toss onto the bed, rolling with thunder, quaking in the dark. There is a drunkenness of youthful infatuation in them, unmatched by any substance in its power to intoxicate and destroy. It is in this motel that CARMEN first beds another carnally, and she suspects it is the first time for AJA, too. Neither of them pays significance to this now.

CARMEN   I love you.
AJA   Yes.

And neither of them will pay significance to this later, when what happens this night will bury emotion and truth.

HAILEY PIPER

Enter older CARMEN, crawling from beneath the bed, clutching a mask that resembles BLANCA. She tries, as she has before, to blot out AJA with the mask as if they are heading to the golden masquerade. If she remembers BLANCA in this part of the night, then she'll know that detail is wrong. And if one part of the night is wrong, it throws the entire night into question, and she can dismiss the memory before it reaches the later part of the night. And what she will feel and say then.

    CARMEN   You're mine.
    AJA   Yes.

But AJA is fire incarnate, and her skin burns the BLANCA mask, sending older CARMEN skittering back under the bed. AJA is the one who made it clear, the day young CARMEN caught AJA secretly kissing her last girlfriend the way girls usually kiss boys, and CARMEN realized you could do that. Not a confusing yet intense fascination with older celebrity women on TV—a direct understanding. AJA was the one who stoked CARMEN'S heart. Who made it feel okay. The one who stood holding CARMEN'S hand and never letting go despite a mother's shouting blame at an absent father, and disgust at a presumed lack of grandchildren, and promises that she will kill herself if her daughter CARMEN does this to her. AJA is the one who makes none of that feel real.

    CARMEN   And I'm yours.
    AJA   Yes.

A GAME IN YELLOW

And AJA keeps that moment unreal, so long as she kisses CARMEN, holds CARMEN, and sits up in the night to watch CARMEN drift into dream.

    CARMEN   No, no.

But eventually AJA must sleep. Must slip away herself, into her own dreams that CARMEN will never know, interrupted when realization crushes CARMEN'S soul and wakes her in a panic during the last thundering remnants of the storm.

CARMEN	I knew she wouldn't be okay. She couldn't be.
AJA	Hush. It's fine. She could have understood. She chose not to.
CARMEN	Because of me. I'm all wrong. She had a whole plan for me.
AJA	And you planned to have two parents together, didn't you?
CARMEN	They couldn't choose me, and I shouldn't be like this.
AJA	No.
CARMEN	I wish I was different. I should be different. Why couldn't I be what she wanted?
AJA	Because you're what I want. This is who you are. You were born to be you, not somebody else, so don't wish you were anyone but you.
CARMEN	Then I shouldn't have been born at all!

AJA	No.
CARMEN	(breaking into sobs) There shouldn't be a me. There should be somebody else, not me. I don't want to *be*. I don't—

AJA coils her limbs around CARMEN as if she can squeeze out the self-loathing. CARMEN cries deep into the night, into sleep. Her denial of truth, of self, is so fervent that it seeds doubt inside AJA too, who wishes she could forget the later part of the night. And maybe forget the night entirely.

Morning. AJA has disappeared from the motel room. She waits in her car to bring CARMEN home. CARMEN does not remark on this. She feels amusedly embarrassed over some half-remembered behavior instead of ashamed, and then she only remembers that feeling—

CARMEN	(laughing) Okay.

—disconnected from any particular memory. Like none of it happened. When CARMEN returns home, she and her mother silently agree to ignore the prior night and never speak of it. The silence aids in the forgetting. CARMEN and AJA do not speak again, passing in school with eyes downcast. They share a look of mutual acknowledgment upon their graduation that they once knew each other, and then they never see each other again. A summer of pretending passes at home until CARMEN finds work in another town, and another, and then in time leaves for the city. The

A GAME IN YELLOW

goodbye to her father is brief. The goodbye to her mother is longer. They, too, never see each other again.

And without a word spoken, CARMEN tells herself it is better this way. Only when presented with the irresistible does she fall entirely into memory.

For the worst truths are of the self.

20

The Rite of Command

CARMEN SNAPPED TO SITTING UP on the couch and hurled the pages away. "Fuck you!"

She had come home in triumph from the office, ready to read. No preparation this time, no expectation, only a hope that *The King in Yellow* would do right by her after spreading the good word and the Yellow Sign. That it would show her further insight into Blanca. Her past.

Instead, it had shown something much more intimate, coiled within a nightmare.

Carmen watched the Act II pages float, crash into each other, and fall to the living room floor. They belonged wrinkled in the copy machine at work. Or the paper shredder.

"It's not some irresistible truth," Carmen whispered. "It's all wrong. Nothing happened like that!"

But that night came back to her, cast like a shadow across her mind by those sun-yellow pages.

Only our sun, Carmen thought. *Not the black suns.*

She rubbed at her face and found tears slicking salt over her fingertips. Aja—right. It hadn't been Blanca that night, couldn't have been, too long ago for when Carmen had tried coming out to her mother, thinking honesty would bring them closer together. Her father had been apathetic, his usual. Her mother had been a tempest. Carmen hadn't called either of them in years she wouldn't count.

Ordinarily, you read the words, Smoke had said when first showing Carmen the play. *But these pages? They read you, too.*

That scene in the play—that wasn't a night Carmen had ever shared with Blanca. They each had awful memories of how their families handled those moments, and they each understood and respected the necessary distance.

There was no respect in these ugly pages. This cursed play.

If Carmen were to bring the pages back to work and put them through the paper shredder, then find the copies she'd made and do the same to them, that might end it. Their fragments might regenerate, but she didn't think so. Not on their own. Her stolen pages had only started growing new sheets after she read them. Same as any writing, the letters were powerless without a human mind to absorb them.

Carmen gathered up the pages and stuffed them back into her tote bag. There could be no reasoning with the King. Time to put an end to this. If Smoke had some machination behind it all, Carmen wouldn't be part of her game. And if the play had its own designs, it wouldn't be able to reach Carmen for much longer.

A GAME IN YELLOW

"There's no such thing—" Carmen started. Swallowed. Tried again. "There's no such thing as Aja."

Locks slid in the apartment door, and Carmen turned around as Blanca pushed her way inside, fussing with her purse.

The keys clattered when Blanca at last looked up. "God, you scared me."

"Sorry." Carmen squeezed her tote bag's strap. "I should be at work, but—"

"No, not that," Blanca said, waving over Carmen's head. "It looked like someone else was here for a second, someone taller."

Carmen shivered.

"Guess it was sunlight in the windows." Blanca pressed the door shut, kicked her shoes off, and dropped her purse on the kitchen counter. "Still not feeling well?"

Right, Carmen had been a mess last night. Both the way Blanca and Smoke thought at first, and the way she'd revealed her messiness later. But if anyone could help, it was Blanca. She'd worried over Carmen's obsession with the play already, over its effect on Carmen and her dreams. Maybe Blanca could do what Carmen couldn't.

"Blanca. What you were saying before, about the play—"

Bright pain stabbed through Carmen's head, a blade of light cresting the horizon of her eyeball. The apartment tilted, and every surface turned a sickly yellow.

All the stage is a shroud except for he of the yellow mantle.

STRANGER   Quiet, Pet.

All the world's a stage, all the stage is an apartment.

Carmen's vision snapped back to Blanca's face, her forehead wrinkled in worry and her lips going up and down, her voice muffled. She clutched Carmen by the shoulders, easing her onto the couch.

"—armen? Carmen, can you hear me?"

Carmen blinked furiously. Her vision blurred again, this time with tears, and she kissed Blanca's cheek, almost an apology. There would be no telling her. That time had passed, and now someone else held Carmen's leash.

"We need a doctor, huh?" Blanca asked.

"No." Carmen wiped at her eyes. "I haven't had any water today. Probably dehydrated."

Blanca's expression shifted, disbelieving, but she marched to the kitchen anyway as Carmen cleared her eyes. Believing or not, Blanca cared about Carmen. Looked after her. They had started this nightmare of Smoke and her vicious play because Blanca's nurturing demeanor wouldn't let Carmen sabotage their relationship.

She had to get her head straight. Mend the disconnect inside her in a way that didn't involve Smoke or *The King in Yellow*. Commit herself to Blanca's quirks and kinks and that bottomless love, a thirst never quite quenched.

Someone like Blanca deserved a partner who'd do anything for her. Between Blanca and *The King in Yellow*, the choice was obvious.

Carmen needed to make it right. Time to reassert who was in command of this game.

"I need to head back to the office, and then I'll be home," Carmen said, rising from the couch and grabbing up her bag again. "But we should do something tonight. Make it special."

A GAME IN YELLOW

"Are you cooking?" Blanca asked, returning with a glass of water.

Carmen drank half of it and set it down on an end-table coaster. "I'll grab dinner on the way home. But also . . ." She let her voice trail, hoping to stoke anticipation in Blanca's furnace.

Blanca's cheeks reddened. "Also?"

"I want to play tonight," Carmen said.

She waited for last night's reluctance. For Blanca to turn surly and finally break up with her, maybe stomp Carmen's heart to fragments in the process.

But a smile lit Blanca's face instead. "Sounds delicious." Blanca kissed above Carmen's ear. "Dinner and dessert."

"Exactly. Just you and me."

Blanca went still beside her. "No Smoke, you mean."

"I want us to play," Carmen said. "Nobody else."

"Do you not like Smoke?" Blanca asked. "She likes you. She wants you to like her, too."

"I do." It wasn't a lie, but Carmen couldn't divide Smoke from her leatherbound demon, not yet. Maybe in time, after she'd reestablished her subservience to Blanca.

Disappointment haunted Blanca's eyes. "You seem jealous. I don't like it."

"Don't you want to make this work?" Carmen asked.

A twitch unsettled Blanca's composure. Something was breaking inside her, and Carmen had to remind herself that Blanca had involved Smoke *specifically* to make this work. First to resolve Carmen's dying sexual enthusiasm, and then to share the burden of her appetite.

And Carmen didn't seem to appreciate any of it. Was she already too late to save their relationship? No, she wouldn't accept that. She needed to change tactics, from the girlfriend making demands to the pet needing attention—no, worse than that.

She needed to be a brat.

"You and Smoke had time, just the two of you," Carmen said, trying to sound alluring. Her fingers wandered Blanca's hair. "Don't I get that, too? A little you-and-me time. Isn't that okay?"

Blanca should have raised her eyebrows and looked aghast at her unfairness. Carmen's guilting should have worked. Telling truths, even unpleasant ones of jealousy and pettiness, meant Blanca had no ulterior motives to detect.

But Blanca only nodded in half-hearted surrender. "All right, Pet. You and me."

Carmen bit the inside of her cheeks not to react. This was worse than infatuation with Smoke and bigger than the game. Something was deeply wrong with their relationship.

Because of me. Carmen hoped that was her thought and not someone else's.

It lined up with what she believed. Carmen was the broken partner, the disconnected one, and yet through it all, Blanca had kept her. How long did Carmen believe this dedication could last? Clever Blanca. Caring Blanca.

But also *human* Blanca. She could get a better girlfriend if she wanted. At some point, she must've started slipping away, and who had been there to cloud around her?

Smoke. The unbroken woman, whose book of truths had pushed Carmen further away.

If Smoke had more to do with the play than ownership, she might have shown it to Carmen for purposes Carmen couldn't imagine.

A GAME IN YELLOW

And if Smoke wasn't entwined with *The King in Yellow*? What then? Worse conclusions. Bad enough for Carmen not to deserve Blanca, to know she could *hurt* Blanca. Carmen had suspected those possibilities for some time.

But for Smoke to come along, this threat of a woman who might not only lack these weaknesses but possibly be good for Blanca? What was Carmen supposed to do with that? Smoke had dangled the play and thrown it for Carmen to play with while she slipped in to entice Blanca with the new, the wild, the unbroken.

No more.

"This won't fix things by itself," Carmen said.

Blanca had returned to the kitchen, but now she glanced over her shoulder, despondent yet curious.

"I'll go to therapy," Carmen went on. "I'll find out what's going on inside me, what's wrong or broken. I promise, I'll put in the work. But I need to belong to you."

Blanca parted her lips. Closed them. Managed something like a smile, both sad and hopeful.

That would have to be good enough for now while Carmen set other matters to rights. There would be healing, and togetherness, and a future. The game would tie them back together, in every meaning Carmen could think up. She would remind herself who mattered in life, remind Blanca who she loved, and Carmen would show that love in return through unparalleled trust.

And she would have to hope tonight wasn't too late.

21

The Fantasy

The golden masquerade settles toward its finale, and the commotion outside has lulled in the way of nocturnal insects quieting when starving birds swoop close. CARMEN has traded the arm of THE STRANGER for that of CASSILDA. Both women dance as if not wholly comfortable, feeling each other out, but there are appearances to maintain while the suns have yet to set.

CARMEN	I should have convinced your Stranger to dance.
CASSILDA	Oh?
CARMEN	Others know of my intended. They would see nothing amiss about a dance with a man.

CASSILDA   Is he a man? That mask appeared as strange shapes to me.
CARMEN   There is someone beneath the mask.
CASSILDA   Or no one. Until the Hour of Unmasking, we can be anyone. You dance with a hawk.
CARMEN   My intended would wonder.
CASSILDA   I was once subject to such whims. You must not know the tale, A Lover from—

CASSILDA pauses to puff out her chest.

CASSILDA   (singing) Carcosa.

CAMILLA slides past, arm in arm with another dancer.

CAMILLA   She dominates the art of discretion.
CARMEN   You two behave as if there is only the masquerade, forever. I worry about us. Don't you sense that dreadful atmosphere? Something is amiss outside.
CASSILDA   Outside? Or in you?

~

The railcar quaked over the tracks, jostling Carmen from sleep. Her window had turned dark. Tangled wires and concrete tunnel walls whisked past the grimy glass, and then the railcar door opened onto a subway platform lined with weary commuters.

The wrong platform. Carmen's dream had made her miss her stop, far enough that she'd ended up underground, as if the

A GAME IN YELLOW

source of the dreams were determined to keep her from righting her wrong.

But she had lived in this city for years, and this wasn't her first instance of having to loop back after missing her stop. Even with the lost time, Liza wouldn't have closed the office yet.

Carmen would run around the office, gathering copies from wherever they'd drifted with *Carmen's Diet* scrawled at the top. She would then stuff those and their mother copy through the paper shredder. Page by page or all at once, and no half measures like that French priest of decades past, tearing the play in half as if that could solve anything.

The only remaining copy would be Smoke's incomplete set of pages, and she was protective of it. So long as she never trusted anyone, and Carmen supposed that would be easy if she ever revealed her theft, then everything would end in shredded strips of yellow.

Carmen reached the office twenty minutes later and popped her head in the breakroom—no one inside, but a partial Act II of *The King in Yellow* remained. Someone had left crumbs on its first page.

The office beyond the breakroom lay silent. No one in the cubicles, no Liza behind her desk. The restroom was empty, too. Everyone had disappeared as if spirited away to the Catskills a few days ahead of schedule, except without locking up, turning off the lights, even shutting down their computers, like none of that mattered anymore.

Maybe it never had.

Same as the Act II copy from the breakroom, the one Carmen had left on her desk lingered, and someone had likewise flipped through its scant pages. She checked the copy room in case anyone had duplicated it, but if they had, they'd taken the new copies with them.

Carmen curled her shaking fist around the clumped pages. She then left the copy machine and planted herself in front of the paper shredder, where she raised the ream of pages—stolen originals, spontaneous new ones, machine-made copies—and jammed them into the shredder's waiting maw. It grunted complaints. They almost sounded like a familiar voice.

"Enough," Carmen snapped. "Enough! I don't want you, or your cities or kings or masks! Leave me alone. Leave Blanca alone. Just leave us the hell alone."

She couldn't be certain whether she was talking only to the play or also to Smoke.

And she also wasn't sure anymore if there was much distinction.

She closed her eyes, nervous the pages might trick her into reading, pull her into a dream, or worse, a memory, and then she shifted them into the shredder. It had no choice but to accept them.

Satisfying yellow slivers curled into the shredder's plastic basin. Each page became a nest of trapped snakes desperate to twist around and mate, but these strips would not be reproducing. No one could read them now. Carmen tried to discern even a single word, but there was nothing.

Because each sliver was a blank sheet of thin black lines.

Notebook pages. Ordinary goddamn yellow notebook pages. The office stocked them in the supply cupboard in the copy room's corner, but Carmen didn't remember picking them up. Same as she had no recollection of stabbing the playroom wall or destroying the mermaid art print's frame.

A GAME IN YELLOW

But she knew what was to blame. The corner of a page from *The King in Yellow* peered out of her tote bag.

Carmen shrieked, lugged the bag to the restroom, and ripped the pages over the open toilet. Tear lines split the Stranger's dialogue markers from his dialogue, the Act numbers from their scenes, and Cassilda's Song into half stanzas and nonsense. Paper flakes poured like limp confetti into the open toilet. Carmen could only hope the disgrace washed all sovereignty from any titular king, Hastur or otherwise.

When she looked into her tote bag again, there were no pages looking back at her. She flushed the toilet, and the remains were gone.

The pages couldn't have weighed much, but she felt lighter as she reached the street, like she'd been carting around a tree trunk and had finally offloaded it in the least-dignified way she could imagine. No more influence. The ordeal was nearly over.

At the 40th Street station, Carmen spotted Liza standing on the above-street platform. Noticing her would've been hard in most any churning afternoon crowd, except that crowd had retreated from her as if her skin carried an infectious disease.

Not her skin, Carmen thought. *Her mind. Her dreams.*

Liza stood panting over the prone body of an elderly woman in a beanie and ragged coat. Red blotches stained Liza's oncewhite blouse. Her hands dripped the same color, and a vicious shard of glass formed a crooked dagger rising spire-like from her grasp. She kicked at the woman, a blank look in both their eyes, but she didn't lash out with her glassy blade.

She'd already carved exactly what she wanted in the dead woman's chest. Carmen saw it clear through the crowd.

The Yellow Sign.

"Need to get back to the real world," Liza said, panicked. "You think that's the sun up there? Just one? Use your heads! This is fantasy. Need to get back. Get to the real world."

A train horn sounded from the east, and Liza swiveled to face the tracks. Onlookers parted, wary of her glass dagger, some holding phones aloft, but Liza wouldn't mug for their cameras. Her head tilted, listening to the train.

And then she started forward.

Carmen retreated down the platform steps, bumping into busy commuters and uncaring tourists. The stairway's top hid the murder scene as she descended, and then the platform entirely, and her gaze fell to her hands. The worst they'd done under the play's spell was stab a wall. Never a person.

Only because Smoke had fed Carmen bits and pieces, letting her taste the play without truly consuming it. Never letting it consume her. A choice she hadn't given to Liza and the office women. Nothing could have stopped their being claimed by a king.

Again the train horn sounded, racing above the streets, its brakes shrieking toward the 40th Street platform. Carmen whirled around and charged for the sidewalk. Better to take the long walk of getting to Queensboro Plaza on foot.

The sounds of commotion rumbled from the platform as Carmen reached the bottom of the steps, and a chorus of screams chased her onto the street.

Every step fell heavily. The curb seemed ready to crumble away, feeding Carmen and other nearby pedestrians into the street, more bodies to toss in front of fast-moving machines.

A GAME IN YELLOW

But the concrete didn't have to do anything. That monstrous domination had crept into Liza's head and let her bring destruction to herself.

Because of Carmen. The company's owners could cancel their synergistic workshop in the Catskills. Call it mandatory all they pleased, only Carmen would be capable of attending. *The King in Yellow* had emptied the office. Wasn't that a kind of synergy? Her coworkers had all done it together, and it hadn't cost the company more than a few pages of printer paper and a squirt of ink.

Carmen's breath halted somewhere between the wind and her lungs, a sense of plastic film covering her trachea. She tried to inhale, exhale, but nothing moved. Dark clouds filled her head, crowding out her thoughts, and a fire lit in her chest. Her fingers tore between her lips, seeking the suffocating plastic.

Her throat was clear. There was nothing to stop her from breathing. She pulled her fingers free and sucked in stale city air, breaking the sense of smothering death. The clouds seeped from her mind.

She couldn't do this to herself. Couldn't take on the weight of her office right now, especially not to a lethal degree. No matter what happened, Carmen had to keep up these simple requirements of living, moment by moment. She'd already managed to keep breathing. She needed sustenance, too. And love. Especially love. If she kept her perspective of the world down to these simple needs, she could make it through anything.

She would pick up dinner on the way, reach home, head upstairs, and fall under Blanca's hands. Her will. That would be the end of the king's reign over Carmen.

She belonged to Blanca now. No one else.

22

The Yellow Safeword

CARMEN PICKED UP SALVADORIAN TAKEOUT in foam containers from a place near Queensboro Plaza for dinner. She kept herself focused only on breathing, and walking, and getting the food, but she realized the moment she reached home that she and Blanca wouldn't be eating until later.

The apartment lay shrouded in darkness, the curtains drawn over every window. Candles flickered from the kitchen countertop, the living room shelves, even from the playroom, where a dark silhouette watched from the doorway. Somewhere, Blanca's phone played an unhurried rhythm at low volume, filling the gloom with gentle percussion, subtle guitar strings, and lilting vocals, their lyrics both indiscernible and unimportant. The mood was all that mattered.

Tremors rocked Carmen's hands. She remembered this

nervousness from her early days with Blanca. A good sign, then. A fresh beginning.

Carmen stuffed the food into the fridge to be microwaved later and then stepped into the living room. Deeper in the candlelight, she found the couch pushed back, and her rope-and-sweat-weathered chair stood alone, a waiting island. Carmen and Blanca hadn't used it since their last breathplay game. Since before Carmen first read from *The King in Yellow*.

Enough—she wouldn't think about that anymore. Only Blanca. Only love and the game.

"You're overdressed," the playroom silhouette said, sultry and commanding. "Wear less."

Carmen unbuttoned her top and slid it from her arms and shoulders. Her slacks went next, crumpling to her knees and then ankles, where she realized she'd forgotten to slip off her shoes.

"Naughty Pet," Blanca said.

"Yes," Carmen said in a rushed gasp.

Out of her shoes, socks, slacks, and then she wriggled her underwear off and approached the chair. Leather cuffs waited at the ankles, but nothing hung from the arms. What did Blanca have in mind?

"Sit, Pet."

Carmen eased onto the chair with a serene smile. Time to be reclaimed. Let Blanca see Carmen's need through the dimness and smell it off Carmen's skin.

The silhouette emerged from the playroom wearing a sleek black robe, its sheen catching and devouring reflections of flickering candlelight. Another outfit hid underneath, a surprise to be revealed later. Carmen would wait as commanded. She'd played the brat earlier. Now she would play the bound angel.

A GAME IN YELLOW

"So, Pet wants attention." Blanca knelt to cuff Carmen's ankles to its legs, her robe forming a black lake beneath her. "I can give you attention. More than you ever dreamed."

She stood then, reached into her robe, and led a white snake of rope into her hands.

Carmen gritted her teeth. Was that the rope she'd cut from her arms this morning? Couldn't be. She'd destroyed that one and—what had she done with the pieces? She couldn't remember, but they were severed beyond usage. This rope looked intact. Either it was a different piece or she'd only imagined cutting herself loose.

Forget it, she told herself. *Doesn't matter. It's over.*

Blanca circled the chair again, letting the rope slide over Carmen's lap, a curious finger tasting everything it touched. Carmen writhed in her seat, impatient like never before. Blanca disappeared behind her.

And then a hand closed around Carmen's forearm and led it over her head and across the upper back of the chair. The other arm followed, and the rope curled around them. First in careful loops encircling her forearms, and then another set of loops around her wrists, and then a handcuff knot. Further tight loops forced her hands to clasp. The rope then descended the back of the chair, where Blanca anchored it between the hind legs, binding Carmen's arms overhead.

Muscles went taut down Carmen's sides and chest. This was dangerous—people had crucified themselves with the wrong binding. But this was also trust, and that was part of the game's purpose.

Even better, bound hands could not stab a screwdriver through a wall.

Blanca appeared at Carmen's front again, one arm stretched past her head, and she gave the rope a playful tug, wrenching a pleased gasp from Carmen's throat.

"Awful noisy." Blanca started for the playroom. "I have just the thing. Be right back."

Carmen nodded, tingling all over. Not with numbness. Something else, the word gone dripping down her chest and pulsing between her thighs.

Blanca called from the playroom doorway. "I was saving this for your birthday, but it sounds like you need it now."

She emerged into the living room again, something dangling from her hand. Candlelight licked at silicone as if tasting it ahead of Carmen—a black ball gag, clinging to leather straps meant to wrap around a face.

Carmen's face. *Yes, do it*, she thought. *I'm yours.*

She'd said those words years ago, to someone else, but she didn't want to think about that. She only wanted this night, right now.

Blanca returned to Carmen's front, grinning. "All right, let's—" Her words fell away as her mouth dropped in a stammering gasp. "Die—die—"

Carmen furrowed her brow. "Blanca? What's wrong? Are you trying to say—"

Blanca raised a quivering hand and snapped her fingers once. Scenario over. She gaped down at Carmen's lap as if her mons had grown a face above vulval lips.

"What's that doing there?" Blanca rasped.

Carmen clenched her teeth. Hated to look down. Looked anyway.

Stiff yellow pages stood against her inner thighs, parting at the center like an open book with her sex as its seam. Carmen couldn't read the words from this angle.

But she knew exactly what these pages were. What would be written on them.

"How did you get them there?" Blanca asked, gaze now darting over her knots.

"I didn't," Carmen said. "It's not like I could give birth to them."

Blanca stomped her foot. "There's no one else here!"

Carmen wasn't sure that was true. There was the Carmen she became in sleepwalking. And there was someone hidden behind plaster and light, holding dominion over her.

"This is what I was trying to warn you about the other night," Carmen said. "You have to make me yours. You have to hurt me!"

Blanca shrank back. "You're scaring me."

"I'm the one tied to a fucking chair!" Carmen bucked. "Cut the pages up. Burn them. I don't want them anymore."

"You want everything," Blanca said, her teeth clenched. "You got bored, so I learned new tricks. Precautions ruined your immersion, so I tamped them down. The ordinary world wasn't cutting it, so Smoke pulled out her secrets. It's never enough. I do so damn much for you, Carmen, but you're asking for more than I can give."

Carmen watched, waiting for Blanca to grab the pages and get their tattered edges off her skin.

But Blanca didn't move. Like this wasn't her problem because these weren't her pages.

"Is that what you're upset about?" Carmen asked. "That Smoke isn't here?"

Blanca glanced away. "You're not listening."

Carmen studied Blanca's profile. She had long wanted more people to appreciate Blanca's beauty, and maybe she'd gotten her wish. Not listening was different from not paying attention.

"That night you introduced me to Smoke," Carmen said. "Was that really the second time you met her?"

Blanca's attention cut back to Carmen, eyes wide with surprise.

"No, then." Tension ached down Carmen's tied arms. "You were talking to her already."

Blanca said nothing.

"How long? Weeks?" More nothing. "Months?"

"Just as friends," Blanca said.

"At the bar?" Carmen asked.

"The club. Raspberry Swirl."

Carmen frowned. "I thought you stopped going."

"With you," Blanca said. "I stopped inviting you because you never wanted to come, but that's still where my friends used to hang out. Where do you think I learned these different knots? I had to keep up with ways to please you."

Carmen's back went flush with the chair. "You could've told me."

"I did, Carmen. But you don't listen. You're pretty terrible at it. Besides, you hated that place, and you weren't sorry the other night to see it gone. If I'd told you that was where Smoke and I met, you wouldn't have given her a chance."

A moment's silence snaked between the dancing candle flames, filling the room with flickering dread. The music was dead. Blanca's phone playlist must have glitched out.

"Do you love her?" Carmen asked.

A GAME IN YELLOW

"I don't know yet," Blanca said, softer. "I'm still figuring this out. But it's serious enough that I wanted to involve you."

"Are you leaving me?"

"I hope not."

Carmen flinched as if doused with a bucket of ice water.

A haunted look weighed at Blanca's features. "I think Smoke is who we're missing. She can hold this together. She knew I was with someone but open to a third. We started talking kink, and became friends, and I got to confiding."

"About me?" Carmen asked.

"Not by name, at first," Blanca said. "We were sidestepping, feeling things out. I told her that some subs get desperate for the fantasy to feel real. That some of them don't understand the responsibility it puts on the dominant partner. It's heavy. And terrifying. What if I screw up? I could really hurt you, Carmen. Not just a dislocated shoulder or a bruise, but *really* hurt you because you don't know when's enough playing."

Another silence fell between them. Even the city held its breath, absent of its usual sirens, car horns, and distant construction.

"If you're so scared, why not break up with me?" Carmen asked.

"Because I'd do anything for you, don't you get that?" Blanca snapped. Her arms thrashed at her sides, and the ball gag's straps clacked against her wrist. "Because I love you for some goddamn reason, you brainless bitch."

"Then take me." Carmen tried bucking the yellow pages out from between her legs, but her sweat must have stuck them to her skin. "If it's got me, then help me. Be patient with me, like always."

"Like always," Blanca echoed. She paced away, muttering something under her breath, and then spun back to Carmen. "That's exactly the thing. It's *always*. Haven't I been patient with you? Like the world crushing a rock into a diamond. I don't know if I still feel the same or, or—"

"If your heart's too hard?" Carmen asked. "If I'm too hard to love? Too much?"

"Too much, and not enough."

Carmen's chest caved into a black hole behind her sternum. She'd known she was a problem, too much to handle, giving not enough of herself, since adolescence. Since Aja.

But it had taken today, and the play, to remind her. Had she grown up at all since then? Even now, an itch inside told her to run as fast as possible away from this nightmarish conversation, and only the miracle of being bound to this chair kept her from doing exactly that and breaking Blanca's heart, same as she'd broken Aja's long ago.

"This is good," Carmen said. "You're letting me see the ugly side. There's always a presentation with you."

"Presentation," Blanca echoed. "You think I'm acting."

"Presenting. You want me to see the best of you, always, looking like you're put-together and perfect, ever since we met, but you're just like me. A mess, Blanca. You have to be." Carmen fought back tears. "So we're the same. And I'm yours. I'll do everything you want."

"Carmen." Blanca said it like a curse. "My heart isn't a game."

"You don't understand what's happening to me," Carmen said. "If you had read *The King in Yellow*—"

"Shut up, Carmen."

A GAME IN YELLOW

Blanca's lips peeled back from her teeth in rage, but an ache filled her eyes. Like she'd never known heartbreak until she met Carmen Mancini.

The pained look vanished as Blanca headed for the kitchen.

"Wait." Carmen tugged her arms again, trying to lower them to her front. They weren't hurting yet, but she doubted she could free herself. "What about me?"

Blanca turned, robe swirling around her legs, and stormed toward the chair. "You don't need me to help you."

She leaned close enough to kiss Carmen's lips. Carmen almost thought that would happen.

But then Blanca's hands rose to Carmen's mouth, and her thumbs wedged the ball gag between Carmen's teeth, squeezing against the roof of her mouth and burying her tongue beneath silicone. The straps spiderwebbed over her face and around the back of her head, quickly tightening beneath Blanca's deft fingers.

"You don't need me to fuck you," Blanca said, her tone going cold. "You can fuck yourself."

She straightened up, eyes burning, maybe reconsidering, and then she turned to the kitchen again.

Carmen tried and failed to shout her name. Under kinder circumstances, sitting here abandoned, silenced, and restrained while forced to watch Blanca enjoy a candlelit dinner alone would have melted her nerves into frenzied lightning.

But their relationship teetered on the edge of shattering. All because of Smoke and her evil little book. Carmen couldn't let this play out like another game.

She squeezed her clasped hands tighter together until one

fingertip met her thumb. The sound came weak, more like thighs rubbing together than a proper finger snap.

But Blanca froze in place, recognizing what Carmen was trying to do. Safety first, Blanca's rule in every scenario, even when Carmen goaded her into bending it. Abandoning Carmen would not be safe. Worse, if Blanca ignored a safeword of any kind, the betrayal would sink into her heart, and she'd never trust herself again, even if Carmen might deserve watching Blanca walk away.

She started toward Carmen, the fight leaving her. They would talk this through, sort it out. Put these pages to the flame.

"Hang on, B."

Carmen and Blanca glanced at the apartment door. It hung slightly ajar, the crack too narrow to let in hallway light and spoil the mood Blanca had worked hard to grow before *The King in Yellow* ruined it.

The source of that play's presence in their lives now pressed the door open wider and shut it behind her. Carmen was distracted on coming home and clearly forgot to lock it.

How long had Smoke been eavesdropping?

"God," Blanca whispered, and then she hurried into Smoke's arms.

Smoke held her. "This doesn't have to be your call."

Carmen grunted, but neither Blanca nor Smoke looked at her. Their voices dropped to forceful whispers, heads rising and tilting to speak and listen. Both women seemed to drift as if Carmen's chair had fallen into a river, carrying her away.

At the end, Blanca's voice climbed loud enough to hear. "But don't leave her tied up alone. People die that way."

"Right," Smoke said. "You're the one who put her in the chair."

"She likes the chair. She likes all of it." Blanca lowered her head, despondent. "All right."

What was all right? Carmen watched Blanca approach, eyes downcast. *Look at me.*

But Blanca didn't glance Carmen's way, refusing to read any thoughts in her covered face or desperate eyes. She headed for the bedroom, hugging herself, and disappeared from sight. The slamming door shot a chill through Carmen. She hadn't felt so alone since—

Aja.

And yet Carmen wasn't alone. Smoke loomed ahead, the candlelight painting pretty shadows and golden reflections over her skin and contours. Her eyes sharpened with menace as she turned to Carmen. And the pages between her legs.

She did not look surprised to see them.

23

Strange Is the Night

SMOKE DRAGGED A CHAIR SCREECHING from the kitchen tiles to the carpet at Carmen's front, where she sat down and crossed her arms and legs over an outfit of black and violet. Her satchel smacked the floor beside the chair. Carmen couldn't help glancing, as if a yellow-paged book might crawl from its darkness.

Or a yellow-mantled figure with pale hands and a nothing face.

"We have a problem," Smoke said. "A couple of problems. And I'm not sure where to start. Because there's this." Her tattooed fingers gestured to the pages between Carmen's thighs. "And then there's how I showed up right as you two were breaking each other's hearts."

Carmen sighed through her nose. Smoke's stolen pages lay right here, and taking them wouldn't reveal anything she hadn't already seen of Carmen. She could have them. Get it over with and leave instead of dragging Blanca into this.

But Smoke didn't look at the pages now. Her stare fixed like a knife into Carmen's face. "I don't see love when I look at you, girl. I see a reptile, everything primal. Blanca deserves to be loved right, and you know that, but can you do it? Blanca has a good eye for people's subtle tics. Especially yours. Don't you think if you wanted a forever with her that she'd have seen it in your face? She wants to be a bride someday."

Carmen already knew that. An angry grunt slid around the silicone.

Smoke traced a talon along Carmen's underjaw strap. "That might seem silly to you, but it matters to her. It matters to me. She has a big heart, and no matter what you've thought of third partners before, I'm not some temporary fling. You're not even upset that I make her happy." Her tone darkened. "You're upset that I'm the woman who can prove her family wrong, and you're afraid of being the one who proves them right."

How the hell did Smoke know about that? Blanca couldn't have told her. She wouldn't have shared that with Smoke and not shared it with Carmen, too.

She knows because the play knows, Carmen thought.

"From what I hear, you ran, too," Smoke went on. "Except without good reason."

She should know better because the play knows.

Carmen wasn't sure which way to believe. Maybe Smoke was trying to pretend both ways, or she wanted to keep Carmen guessing. Likely this wasn't some spur-of-the-moment speech. Smoke had been thinking about it for some time, and now she was going to speak her mind.

A GAME IN YELLOW

But Carmen didn't have to listen. She clenched her teeth around the ball and strap, adjusted her hands overhead, and pincered her fingertip and thumb.

Smoke raised an open palm. "Before you snap your fingers, I brought you a present. But I won't show it if you play your get-out-of-jail-free card."

Carmen held still. She could bite down harder, but without the power to slice through in one bite, she would have to chew, and she'd get silicone stuck in her teeth. That seemed like overkill. She could salvage this if she got smart, real quick.

Eyes narrowed, she raised and lowered her chin in a pensive nod. She doubted the present was anything good, but she wanted to see.

Smoke uncrossed her arms and leaned to one side. Spidery fingers teased at her satchel's mouth, but she didn't have to dig far.

The King in Yellow climbed from the satchel. The candlelight cast jittering shadows down its leathery face, suggesting eye sockets, nostrils, mouths, expressions. Carmen's heart banged its fists, that yearn-terror stretching through her body.

"It isn't complete," Smoke said. "But of course, you knew that."

She plucked up the stray pages, briefly exposing Carmen's groin to the living room's fiery glow, before she grabbed a blanket off the couch and tucked it over Carmen's breasts and lap. Carmen didn't care about her nakedness, but Smoke clearly did.

Stop being gentle, Carmen thought. *Stop trying to impress me.*

Smoke cracked open her leatherbound tome and slid the stolen pages inside. "I'll let you keep that Act I you found, wherever it is. One of us isn't a thief." A mean glint sharpened her eyes. "Question for you—if a tree falls in the woods when no one's around, does it make a sound?"

Carmen grunted again, and a thread of saliva leaked past her lower lip.

"What is that? Dimetrodon? Wrong answer." Smoke wiped it away with her thumb, tender as ever. "There's you, demanding greater extremes, and now you've found someone happy to oblige. So, here we are. Another riddle, and you'll remember this one. How is a stage play like a game?"

Carmen swallowed behind the gag and waited.

"Exactly—without players, it is nothing," Smoke said, slowing at the last word. She shut the leathery book and weighed it in her hands. "Somewhere between terror and madness lies ecstasy. Or is it that somewhere between terror and ecstasy lies madness? Maybe terror tells a lie of ecstasy, slowing you down until the madness catches up."

Enough riddles. Carmen shook her head and grunted for Smoke to get on with it.

"Okay, okay." Smoke's talons drummed the leather cover. "I was supposed to visit today, until Blanca told me not to. And I would've steered clear, followed her wishes, but fate intervened about forty-five minutes ago. You've been reading this thing, probably not absorbing much, thanks to your interruptions. Have you heard of the Yellow Sign? Maybe seen it?"

Carmen nodded. She couldn't pretend otherwise. Roddy had mentioned it.

"This afternoon, there was a woman muttering to herself near the park," Smoke said. "*It's a sign*, she kept whispering. Like Roddy, I thought, but I wrote it off. Lots of people have problems in this city. But then there was a train shutdown over a murder-suicide. You can find videos of the aftermath all over online, Carmen. Even the stabbing victim, with her chest carved open in a very particular symbol. And this couldn't have been our boy Roddy—he ran into traffic this morning. It was all over the news. Too early to be responsible for that train platform stabbing." Smoke leaned forward. "So what exactly did you do?"

Carmen's yearn-terror fell into some inner abyss. She snapped her fingers, and then again, and again.

Smoke reached up and closed her talons around Carmen's hands. "That trust is already broken. You changed the rules when you stole from me."

Carmen grunted for Blanca, but she either couldn't hear or didn't care anymore.

Smoke eased back into her seat, still clutching the book. "Roddy. The woman in the park. The platform stabbing. Sometimes people who read the play think they'll go into its world when they die. A fantasy more real than real."

Carmen cocked her head. Smoke couldn't mean only Roddy and Liza. Maybe the office girls, too. Like Natasha.

"Yes, there've been others," Smoke said. "People like you, who got a taste and then a craving. They tell me about black stars, dead cities, and sometimes they paint the Yellow Sign on their walls or scratch it into their skin. I only get so much before they disappear. Before they try to start street armies or underground churches, or kill themselves. Some think they'll die and go to Hastur. Others dream they'll finally cross the Lake of Hali and walk the streets between the golden spires of Carcosa."

Carmen shrank against the seat.

Smoke looked disappointed. "Carmen, it's not real. It just makes you think it is."

She sounded like a mother reassuring a five-year-old against a nightmare. She had no idea, probably hadn't read two lines of the play herself, her catlike curiosity only carrying her so far. It was easier and safer for her to feed the book to other people and glean what she could from their repetitions and ramblings.

"Now, I warned Roddy," Smoke went on. "Like I warned you. But someone else put those women's eyes to these pages. I need to know what you did."

She reached for the back of Carmen's head and unfastened the buckles of her straps. Their leather spiderweb slinked from Carmen's face, and a soft tug freed the silicone ball from her mouth with a wet pop. Smoke walked toward the kitchen to place the gag on the counter.

Leaving *The King in Yellow* on her seat, its pages grinning mustard teeth.

Carmen sucked in a breath and licked her lips. "Dimetrodon."

"I need to know what you did first," Smoke said. She returned from the kitchen and stood behind her chair. "I trusted you, and now we have yellow-tongued freaks loose in the city. I should've known even a taste would be too much."

"Then why let me read it?" Carmen snapped.

Smoke blinked at her, the answer obvious. "For Blanca. We met, got to know each other a little, and your problem came up. I had a solution, and it worked. And then it wasn't enough for you."

Carmen's hands tried to form fists behind her head. Her arms ached, needing to settle, but Blanca's knots wouldn't let go. It would have been a fun evening had *The King in Yellow* kept away.

And Smoke. "I fall hard. It's what I do, and I'm not proud of it. Wild at heart. Love at first sight might be bullshit, but you of all people can appreciate how fascinating she is. The things she finds funny. The care she takes in everything she touches. I swear, it's like a library in her mind. And yeah, she's gorgeous—in the truest sense of the word, you desire to gorge on her beauty—but it wasn't love at first sight. It was love at first conversation."

"I don't want to talk about Blanca with you," Carmen said.

"Of course not." Smoke plucked up the book and stuffed it into her bag. Carmen's insides sagged at its disappearance. "I'd be ashamed if I were you, too. You think that if you can make her own you, then you own her in return. But that's something you have to give. It can't be exchanged. You've run from things before, I can tell, and you want her to trap you. Keep you. Make sure you can't run again."

Carmen parted her lips, about to ask, *How do you know that?*

She stopped herself. Her tongue had betrayed her before, and she didn't want that name, Aja, spilling into the apartment. Besides, Smoke might have tipped her hand. Maybe she did know everything the play knew.

"She loves you, girl," Smoke went on. "Goddamn, she loves you. And you're so distracted, you can't see how vulnerable that makes her. You have your game, but you play with real things too, and people get hurt in ways your tiny Carmen brain can't imagine. Even Blanca. I'm crazy about that woman. She isn't certain about me yet, but she's getting there. You and I don't feel that way about each other, but there's an attraction.

I thought we could make this work. I still do. But you have to open up."

Carmen flinched. "I didn't—" She cut herself off, unsure what she meant to say. *I didn't hurt her*? Or *I didn't mean to*?

"Tell me," Smoke said. "You didn't *what*? Didn't mean to control her? Didn't mean to keep her from running?"

Carmen's voice curdled into a snarl. "And where the fuck did you run from?"

"Me?"

"Yeah. You. Let's read together, Smoke. See what *The King in Yellow* has to say about you. It showed me some of Blanca's past she didn't want to tell. Some of mine I didn't want to remember. What will it show about you that you don't want to share? Like who are you, really? Why are you here?"

Smoke's careful façade flickered. Or maybe that was the candlelight. She looked confused, but Carmen could see through that almost as well as Blanca would have.

"Don't play dumb," Carmen said. "You pass along these stories of traveling, but everyone starts somewhere. Tell me where you began. Where's the fire to you, Smoke? New York? Out west?" She licked her lips. "Carcosa?"

Smoke barked an incredulous laugh, as performatively cheerful as a game-show host. "I don't know what you're talking about. Listen to that paranoia. You're practically drooling it. You can't tell what's real anymore, can you?" She raised a hand. "How many fingers am I holding up?"

Carmen seethed, but she refocused from Smoke's face to her fingers—two. Enough to poke through a mask and spear someone's eyes on those black talons.

A GAME IN YELLOW

But in the dancing candlelight, wasn't their sheen almost yellow?

"You want to know the truth?" Smoke asked. "Maybe I am an inhabitant of Carcosa. The king and I have made a deal. The play wants you. I want Blanca. Everyone's happy." Her head tilted as if it were shrugging. "Or I'm just fucking with you."

"Let me go," Carmen said. "I'll show you what fucking with someone really looks like."

"I bet. You think the play taught you something about life." Smoke nodded at her satchel. "It shouldn't be possible, should it? For a few sheets of paper to damage flesh, blood, our sense of reality. But reality is a flimsy fucking idea. All this?" She rapped her fist against the chair seat between Carmen's thighs. "The solidity is a pageant. Putting on a play for us. We don't realize we can leave that solidity, and we certainly don't expect it to take an intermission, but when you mess with something like *The King in Yellow*, you can't see the illusion anymore. You got up from reality's play to freshen up, and now you're locked out. You have to go to the play across the street now, and it isn't as comforting, or as fun. The players quit performing a show and begin playing a game."

Carmen eyed Smoke's satchel, half expecting the pages to rise in a mustard-colored tornado forming the Stranger, or King Hastur, or to plaster themselves across the ceiling, letting shadows cast by candlelight form the two dark suns above the lake.

Nothing happened. Carmen let out a harsh breath.

"But then, sometimes the solidity is all we have to work with," Smoke said, sounding wistful. "You have to peel it away to reach the secrets. Like what you did. Like the truth you're going to tell me."

Smoke rummaged in her satchel and drew out a familiar black shaft. Carmen had seen it in Rico's, wielded to scare Roddy, and she'd brushed past it when stealing pages from *The King in Yellow*.

Smoke's thumb hit a switch, and serrated steel shot up from her fingers. Candlelight haunted the shiny blade.

"Maybe the truth is deeper than the surface," Smoke said, aiming the switchblade at Carmen. "Maybe I'll find it under your mask."

Carmen shook her head. Her face felt naked. She wished something could shield her. Blanca's leather straps, or a helmet.

Or a genuine mask, pilfered from the golden masquerade.

"Tell me what you did." Smoke dragged the flat of the blade along Carmen's shin, across the cuff that bound her ankle to the chair leg. "If there's no mask, there should be no lies."

The switchblade climbed Carmen's bent knee, her thigh and hip, and skirted the blanket's edge until it crossed the side of her breast, threatening to cut into the fat. Its chill nipped her neck as if stabbing her, and she tensed, hating this, but also easing into it, that survivor's euphoria pounding a lustful itch between her legs. She and Smoke could play a Blanca-made scenario of ropes and knives.

Except Blanca would wipe that away with another *Safety first*. Which meant this moment had to be serious. A game played for keeps.

"Smoke," Carmen whispered. "Forget the book. We can have fun again, right?" Her breath rushed in and out. "Take the blanket off. Mount me, kiss me, get Blanca to come out."

A GAME IN YELLOW

"With you as the center of attention," Smoke whispered. "Vessel for pleasure, the object of our desire."

"Yes. I can be those things. You said it must be nice, someone giving you no choice but to do what you want? It is. That can be us."

"I believe you." Smoke let the blade linger at Carmen's jaw, a journey seemingly finished, and then raised it to Carmen's right cheek. "But people are dead, and I need to know how bad it's going to get."

"*Need*," Carmen echoed. "Or do you want to hurt me, and someone's giving you no choice?"

"Yeah, someone's giving me no choice," Smoke said. "*You*. Now tell me what you did." She leaned toward Carmen's left and kissed the cheek untouched by steel. "Tell me, and maybe we can move past this. We can even learn to love each other."

A doorknob jangled, grasped at by a shaking hand, and then Blanca swept from the bedroom. Tearstains glimmered in the candlelight. How long had she been crying over Carmen?

"I'm sorry." It was the best Carmen could do.

Blanca only bared her teeth. "I don't want your sorry. Just tell her what you fucking did."

The command seized Carmen's heart. No one was going to stop this. Even if she tried screaming, they could wedge the ball gag back into her mouth, turn the TV to blasting. No one in this city cared what happened in some run-down apartment building. Especially not to Carmen.

She swallowed hard, cheek pressing against cold steel.

And then she told Blanca and Smoke what she'd done. In life, in dreams, uncertain which was more real. She told them everything.

24

The Hour of Unmasking

BLANCA WAS CRYING AGAIN BY the end, while Smoke was a statue.

Carmen wished she felt terrible. She wanted to be crying, too, but there was nothing. She'd clawed out the truth, and not even regret would take its place.

"Let me get this straight," Smoke said. "You let one woman stumble into this, and now she's missing. And then you didn't like the unsweetened cornflake girls you worked with, so you not only tore apart their minds but set them loose on the city."

"You did it to that guy," Carmen said.

"Roddy consented. You lured and lied and didn't give them a choice." Smoke sighed, deflating. "Sometimes, among the suicides and religious freaks, the play conjures up a tyrant to spread its word. I couldn't see that in you. The play's dangerous, but I didn't think you would be a danger. But that was before, and now I get it—the whole submission/domination thing. Ever since that night with Roddy, with the pages in the wall. It only looks like Blanca's in charge, but under the illusion, you set the boundaries. You decide you're not to blame."

Carmen glanced to Blanca. She had probably taught Smoke that only recently.

"It's the same here. Abdication of responsibility. Might as well enjoy the high, right?" Smoke's blade trembled at Carmen's cheek, threatening to slice her face away like a mask from her skull. "Submissive little tyrant. Most minds are hard, so they break, but your mind is pudding, and *The King in Yellow* could shape you without destroying you."

Smoke lowered the switchblade and tucked its steel back into its shaft. Not freeing Carmen, but not cutting her either.

"How much of the Carmen we know is left?" Smoke asked. "I warned you. Read too much, and you don't come back."

Carmen almost wanted to laugh. Smoke had it entirely wrong, and she would know that if she could've stood on that rail platform and seen Carmen react to Liza. She would've noticed the difference between them.

"I'm here," Carmen said, determined to sound calm. "Me, like I've always been. You let me read a little at a time. I built up a tolerance. There's nothing to worry about."

"You did? Well, that's great." Smoke leaned back. She didn't look angry anymore, only sad. "I knew a girl who read too much of the play. She was important to someone close, and that made her important to me. But she became obsessed. Dreaming herself into Hastur. Couldn't keep her hands off the pages. She started to see the Yellow Sign, fantasize about figures in yellow, and show the play to other people without warning them. *The King in Yellow* drove her out of her mind."

Carmen gave an uneasy smile. "I promise, that won't happen to me."

A tearful sheen coated Smoke's eyes. "Carmen. Who do you think I'm talking about?"

Blanca turned away and swiped at her face. Carmen flinched to hold her, but the rope bound her in place. Smoke had it wrong. Dreams were brain junk, nothing more.

Except Carmen read the play with the same mind that dreamed. Like any reading, you stared at symbols, or listened to words, or stroked bumps beneath fingertips, and your mind did the work, using the book's information to mold thoughts into fresh concepts. A book that twisted someone's thoughts—it would seem harmless, wouldn't it? How would someone know for certain if their thoughts came from themselves or from some invasive sallow presence?

"No, no, that's not me," Carmen snapped. "What the hell do you know? Have you read even a word of it? Can you even tell if it's a world we touch through the play? Or is it a play that swallowed a world?"

Smoke's sternness flickered with uncertainty.

"Don't act so pure. What about everyone who's fallen for you and then fallen for *The King in Yellow*? You keep it around like that switchblade, like it's something you can control, but it isn't." Carmen chinned at Blanca. "It'll get her, too. Because of us. You're no better than me. He's got a hold on you, too."

"He?" Smoke asked.

"Don't you feel it?" Carmen then chinned at the playroom doorway. "There's someone else here. He's been with us for days. I can show you where he's hiding."

She knew she didn't sound any saner for talking like this, but what else could she do? There was no other explanation. If the book had grabbed Carmen by the mind, it must have done the same to Smoke. She was too careless with it, too trusting. A loaded gun was dangerous, but the worst kind was the one you thought wasn't loaded.

Smoke gave the playroom's candlelit doorway a contemptuous look. She gave the same look to Carmen's binding. Her switchblade danced in her fingers, considering her options.

She then strode behind Carmen's chair and began to drag it across the living room. Every scraping inch brought a grunt up from her throat. The movement was hard effort for her, not as strong as she liked to pretend, and she had to fight the chair in jerking motions little by little.

"You could let me go," Carmen said. "What's the endgame here?"

Smoke didn't answer.

Carmen turned her attention to Blanca. "Is it killing me? A breakup? I don't blame you. You're too good for me."

Tears again welled in Blanca's eyes. "Stop it."

"It knows you're too good," Carmen said. "It's heard that I'm unwanted, so now it wants me. It's what I deserve. But you could give me better than I deserve."

Blanca's features creased, looking offended. "You're not unwanted."

"Then you have to want me. Make me yours before any of

A GAME IN YELLOW

them do. It's Camilla, and Cassilda, and the Stranger, too." Carmen craned her head back to look at Smoke. "And her! Don't let her take me to Carcosa."

"Shut up, Carmen!" Blanca shrieked. She turned to Smoke and spoke in a desperate flurry of Spanish that sounded like questions.

"Don't shut me out," Carmen said.

But neither Smoke nor Blanca looked at her, keeping to their own worrisome conversation, with Smoke fussing the chair over the floor.

"No," Smoke said.

Blanca spoke again, this time in a whisper.

"Because they'll just shoot her!" Smoke snapped. "We're responsible. We have to handle it. Nobody else."

"How?" Blanca asked.

"Here. Right here."

The chair dropped from carpet to floorboards as it screeched through the playroom doorway in jerky movements. Blanca had lit candles along the shelves, intent on creating a romantic atmosphere, but they could only give decent lighting to one half of the room, leaving the rest in an unsteady shadow of intimacy. The flames cast burning eyes off the plastic containers along the shelves. Every art print seemed to dance with uncomfortable distortion, as if opening windows to murky hellscapes. The cushiony bench was a hunching iron cougar at the room's center, holding still only in hopes that one of these three women would let her guard down before it snapped at her limbs. The cardinal walls had darkened to a bloodlike smear.

Blanca followed through the doorway on uneasy steps.

Carmen kicked, straining at her ankle bindings. She could wriggle loose given time, but no way Smoke would let that happen. Not until she was done.

Carmen cast pleading eyes at Blanca. "My arms hurt."

Blanca stared at her, pensive and heartbroken.

Carmen pursed her lips and then mouthed careful syllables. *Die-meh-tro-don.*

Blanca looked away. Regardless of the past couple years, the care, the movie nights, the sex, the love, the devotion, right now she was more unified with Smoke than with Carmen. If it had only been fear, Carmen might have understood.

But Smoke and Blanca were joined in their conviction that Carmen had lost her mind. Only this playroom could prove they were all in this mess together.

The three of them, and what might live in the scarlet wall.

Smoke set the chair at the playroom's center, where Carmen tucked her face against one upraised arm. She didn't want to see, but she couldn't help glancing out the corner of her eye.

Someone had swept up the glass from the mermaid print's frame and returned the frame to the wall, facing inward. Its back reminded Carmen of Liza's desk photos, another darkness looking into her. Had she taken care of the glass this morning? Set the frame with its face to the wall? Blanca would have mentioned if she'd done it, but Carmen had no memory of cleanup. Maybe it was somnambular Carmen, walking through another dream.

Or something in the wall, drawing the lid over its hiding place.

"Under there," Carmen said.

A GAME IN YELLOW

Smoke followed her gaze to the reversed frame. Her shoulders shuddered as her fingers gripped either side, but she held on tight and lifted it from the wall. A flash of its face caught in the candlelight—no mermaid, no lover, only jaundiced skies and a dead shore—before Smoke set it face down on the floor.

Twin stab wounds stared from the scarlet wall, the eyeholes of a plaster mask.

"This?" Smoke asked, aiming a finger.

Carmen nodded.

Smoke laid a hand against the plaster and then recoiled as if she'd touched the flayed muscle of a rotting corpse. "It doesn't feel right." She began to lean, maybe to peer through the stab wounds, making the wall a mask of her own.

Blanca sniffed and then wrinkled her nose. "It smells like stagnant water. A dead pond."

"Or a lake," Carmen said. "Of Hali."

Smoke stood without peering through the eyeholes. "Give me a minute."

Carmen thumped in her chair. "Do you believe me now?"

"It's just writing on a page," Smoke said, sounding lost and uncertain. "Meaningless without someone to read it. Same as all books."

But her curiosity was wrestling with denial, tempted by irresistible truths made manifest. She had to be wondering whether the Lake of Hali, and things from that lake, waited on the other side of this thin plaster, and then maybe the cities of Hastur, Alar, and Carcosa, and all the mysteries of the Hyades.

"It's not stuck in the play," Carmen said. "Something's come through."

Smoke glared at her. She then thumbed the switch of her switchblade's shaft, freeing the steel again, and jabbed it into the wall between the earlier stab wounds. It sank through the plaster, easy as flesh.

Carmen went cold all over. "Smoke, don't. You'll set it free."

Smoke didn't answer. She plunged the switchblade into another spot, and another, perforating the edges of some obtuse shape.

Carmen turned her head. Bad enough this was happening, she didn't want to watch pale hands or golden snakish limbs come crawling through whatever door she'd opened in her sleep.

Her eyes fell on Blanca, standing to one side of the doorway.

"Dimetrodon." Carmen thrust her hips from the chair, making its legs pound the floor, and she snapped her fingers behind her head. "Let me go, Blanca. You have to. I said the safeword. Safety first, remember?"

Blanca rubbed her eyes with the heels of her hands. "I do."

"Then stop this," Carmen said, pleading. "Dimetrodon. Dimetrodon! Please. Cut me loose and I'll leave. You'll never see me again."

"I don't want that," Blanca said. "I want to keep you."

Carmen wanted Blanca to keep her too, but if she had to choose, better to lose the relationship than herself. Beside them, Smoke began to saw at the wall, serrated teeth chewing out powdered plaster.

"It's too late for that," Carmen said.

Blanca crept closer to the chair. "Why?"

A GAME IN YELLOW

A good answer did not exist, but Carmen wanted one. Get Blanca on her side, get herself freed, get away. There had to be something she could say to help herself before that thing in the wall slid loose.

But the sounds of Smoke's cutting shook every excuse out of Carmen's head. The world was sinking into an abyss, and she felt herself descending with it.

"Because I'm nothing, aren't I?" Carmen asked. "Or, I live in nothing."

"You aren't making sense," Blanca said, approaching the chair.

Carmen gazed past her, staring at a nondescript part of the doorframe. "It's like I've spent my whole life wandering in what I thought was an empty cave, and I realized recently that it's some enormous animal's lair. And the harder I tried to get away, the closer I got, and now I'm standing behind the thing. I can finally see how large it is. And how small I am. It hasn't noticed me yet, but it will. A stumbling footstep, a sneeze, a breath too loud. It's only a matter of time."

Tears leaked down Carmen's cheeks. Everyone else had cried this evening; it was her turn. A cracked wailing slid from her lips. The fantasy was dead, maybe her relationship along with it, and her soul, and she needed to escape with whatever she had left before she truly became nothing. Her body trembled as Smoke broke a chunk from the wall.

"Shush, shush," Blanca said, her voice tender, a hand reaching to stroke Carmen's cheek. "It'll be okay."

Carmen's wailing became muffled as she snapped at Blanca's wrist.

She'd closed her teeth around Blanca's flesh before, but only the soft places. Biceps, breasts, neck, belly, even the side of her foot once to hear her shriek and laugh.

But Carmen had never bit into thin sinew before, and never this hard. There was no blaming the play's influence. This was all Carmen. Her animal side, that lizard brain bucking off survivor's euphoria to fight and survive again.

Blanca broke away, screaming. A dark crescent opened her wrist, and Carmen tasted iron on her teeth.

Smoke quit cutting the wall and hurried to Blanca's side. In moments, they would turn on Carmen again. What would come next?

"Let me go," Carmen said. "Get me away from them, away from here."

Her tongue went limp. She wasn't sure if that was panic, or a weird version of subspace, or if she had forgotten how to speak with the taste of her girlfriend's blood in her mouth.

Away from here. Somewhere else. Anywhere.

Her sight blurred through thick tears, and dark clouds wreathed her vision as if she were again asphyxiating in breathplay with Blanca, that plastic sensation kissing her lips. The wall's many wounds stretched and then climbed past the ceiling. Scarlet faded to yellow, the room blooming into a behemoth's maw, and the wounds in the plaster became two again. There were no longer eyeholes, but—

—*twin suns, ever-setting above the Lake of Hali, their reflections undisturbed upon its placid surface.*

"There's a—" Carmen started.

A GAME IN YELLOW

CARMEN   —freedom in letting go.

BLANCA   (speaking calmly) It's all right. I cut ties, like you. My eldest sister did it all, my younger sister needed everything. I looked for love, and I found what—

"—the hell is happening to her?" Blanca asked, unseen. "Carmen?"

"You need a bandage," Smoke said, frantic. "I have to—"

SMOKE   (speaking calmly) —cut loose, too. The road was kinder than where I came from, and there are always places to go.

BLANCA   Absolved of responsibility.

SMOKE   Ceasing to be, and thus becoming.

Enter CARMEN, briefly vanished from the golden masquerade, now returning to the stage and its dancing masked nobles.

BLANCA   Did you dream about me?

CARMEN   (reluctant) Yes.

BLANCA   And was it a nightmare?

CARMEN   Yes.

BLANCA   But you still love me.

CARMEN   Yes. I still love you. But you aren't really Blanca, are you?

BLANCA   Are you really Carmen? Is there such a thing?

At once, the BLANCA and SMOKE masks drop from their wearers, revealing the feline and hawkish masks of CA-MILLA and CASSILDA.

    CAMILLA   It was only another mask, my love. A part of the game.

CARMEN stands with them, no longer naked, once more dressed in her canary ballgown of shining trim and phoenix-like plumage. One hand strokes her wrist, loosened from bindings, and she tastes her teeth, clean of blood. She has come of her own desire, and the jubilance at her freedom becomes obvious in her stride.

The pain will find her later. Pain always finds the one it belongs to.

    CARMEN   Wait, what pain? What does that mean?

Before she can consider what she's asked, she finds CA-MILLA grasping her arm.

    CAMILLA   No longer distracted, my dear? Has your intended driven you away at last?
    CASSILDA   Or have we lured you?
    CARMEN   It's a relief to see you again, my friends. I never ventured to think of this place as a sanctuary.
    CAMILLA   (bemused, aside to Cassilda) Isn't her ignorance charming?

A GAME IN YELLOW

CARMEN flinches.

CAMILLA	A sanctuary is all this place has ever been. The true self emerges once disguised.
CASSILDA	Behind the masks.
CAMILLA	Since the beginning of the masquerade, we have hidden our faces to avoid ourselves and our end, and yet the predator clock circles. Only until the Hour of Unmasking may we frolic.
CASSILDA	And then even the Stranger must unmask.

Around them, the golden masquerade trembles, this last bastion of Hastur buckling from the influence of a world beyond the Hyades. A bell rings in the streets.

CAMILLA	Is it the hour already? I thought we had more time.
CASSILDA	But I suppose time is the prospect of Alar and not Hastur.

CARMEN has no answer. In a kinder play, the audience might now be invited to shout encouragement at the stage.

But there is only the tolling of the last bell of Hastur.

CAMILLA	You, sir, should unmask.
CARMEN	Oh? Me?

CAMILLA waits.

CARMEN	(aside to audience) Am I playing the Stranger?
CAMILLA	(clearing throat and whispering) "Indeed?" Your line is "Indeed?"
CARMEN	Oh. Right. Indeed?
CASSILDA	Indeed it's time. We have all laid aside disguise but you.
CARMEN	Hang on. Do you two know you're in a play?

CAMILLA waits again, impatient.

CARMEN	Or are you pieces of the play that look like people?
CAMILLA	(whispering again) "I wear—"
CARMEN	I know, I know. (deep breath) I wear no mask.
CAMILLA	(terrified, aside to Cassilda) No mask? No mask!
CARMEN	No mask.

CARMEN paws at her face.

CARMEN	I'm sorry. This was a mistake. I shouldn't have come here, and I can't play with you anymore.

A GAME IN YELLOW

CARMEN stumbles up the staircase, her ballgown trailing. A shroud falls over the rest of the stage. Not dimmed—gone as if it has never been.

MOTHER   Cutting ties again.

CARMEN slows her ascent but does not stop.

CARMEN   Mom?

All the dancers become maskless, then faceless, and then shadows reaching for CARMEN. They bear familiar shapes CARMEN doesn't want to see.

AJA	She always stops caring, eventually.
MOTHER	It is her mask, to hide what she is.
AJA	But now what is she?
CARMEN	I wore a mask to this masquerade, right? I stared through its eyeholes. Don't I wear a mask?
MOTHER	When you were small, you'd always tell me you were bored. And I'd tell you that you must be a boring person. You decided to wear a mask to intrigue others, but that did not hide the dullness within. You are exactly the nothing you have always appeared to be.
CARMEN	You're not my mother. Or Aja. You're more pieces of the play.

AJA   These are your irresistible truths. Don't you want them anymore? You can't resist.

CARMEN should reach the top of the staircase, where its left and right sides meet. Instead, the staircase crosses itself and continues to ascend. So does she.

MOTHER   A bored child.
AJA   A dull teen.
BLANCA   A nothing adult desperate for her fantasy to feel real, for the dream to eat her.
SMOKE   An abyss of endless craving.

CARMEN escapes the shadows as the staircases and landings fork, merge, and splay themselves into a towering web above the Lake of Hali. Below, Hastur's music has gone quiet, and Alar lies bejeweled but faint, and Carcosa is brilliant and beautiful and lurking.

CARMEN   Even an abyss can be lonely.

Enter THE STRANGER, rising from a far staircase, carrying his tome, wearing his tattered yellow mantle and pallid mask, facing CARMEN with capricious intent.

CARMEN   You? Then I took up your role by mistake. Where were you during the Hour of Unmasking?

A GAME IN YELLOW

THE STRANGER *begins the labyrinthine journey up and down the winding steps. His garments coil at his feet like a nest of yellow vipers, the cloth prehensile and almost venomous.*

    CARMEN   Are you King Hastur?

THE STRANGER *does not answer. He reaches an adjoining staircase and descends, forcing* CARMEN *to descend as well, ballgown flowing behind her.*

    CARMEN   I don't belong here.

She runs, meaning to quit the game, as she quits everything, only now a pursuer won't let her.

    CARMEN   I don't want to play anymore. I don't want to be part of the play.

The descent is as endless as the abyss inside her. There is no returning to the golden masquerade. That scene of the play has finished without CARMEN. *Her gown pools golden around her, feathers falling. She looks at the twin suns. Or are they stab wounds in a plaster wall? Does someone look through them now?*

    SMOKE   (disembodied) Writing on a page. Meaningless without someone to read it.

CARMEN *raises her pleading hands to the black-eyed heavens.*

CARMEN   Smoke? Blanca? Whoever's there, please stop reading. Something bad is going to happen to me. The animal's noticed, and it wants me, but it can't happen if you stop. Smoke was half right, a game is nothing without players, but a play needs something else—an audience. If there's no audience, it stops right here.

Nothing feels different. THE STRANGER nears.

CARMEN   You're doing this. Right now. End it. Stop reading!

CARMEN loses her voice at the last. Her gaze turns from the suns to her quivering hands. They persist. She persists with them. Has the reading ended? Or is she stuck here, in this once-alluring dream, whether someone reads her or not? Even the players must watch themselves.

And THE STRANGER nears.

CARMEN   (laughing without mirth) Oh. A little trap, set for myself. Cassilda understood.

An echo rises from offstage.

CASSILDA   Strange is the night where black stars rise,
And strange moons circle through the skies,

A GAME IN YELLOW

> But stranger still is
> Lost Carcosa.

CARMEN lowers her hands to her lap. THE STRANGER looms, only a few steps away.

CARMEN   (mesmerized) But stranger still is lost Carcosa.

THE STRANGER has nearly reached her.

CARMEN   But stranger is Carcosa.

THE STRANGER extends a pale hand.

CARMEN   Stranger is Carcosa. The Stranger!

As THE STRANGER almost touches her, CARMEN slides down a few steps, rises to her feet, and whirls around. The twin suns cast her shadow like a giant's silhouette across the Lake of Hali below.

CARMEN	You.
STRANGER	Yes.
CARMEN	I didn't mean to play your role.
STRANGER	But you played it well. You are, indeed, a stranger.
CARMEN	They thought you were the king.
STRANGER	But not of Hastur.
CARMEN	And not a stranger.

STRANGER	The King in Yellow—a moniker delivered by the playwright, a contradiction akin to a city that is called lost while plainly seen across the Lake of Hali.
CARMEN	Stranger still is lost Carcosa.
STRANGER	The soul of it. King and city. As your Arthur of Avalon, as Hastur of Hastur.
CARMEN	(terrified, aside to audience) The Stranger is Carcosa.

THE STRANGER *lengthens, a shadow of Carcosa wearing its darkness and paleness and yellowy nature in every manner until one might believe a city descends the steps, a role of* CARMEN *.*

CARMEN	Why my memories? My mother? Aja?

CARCOSA *opens his book and flips through its pages.*

CARCOSA	They are what I have read of you.
CARMEN	But why?
CARCOSA	For the reason of all readers, to absorb the one I have read.
CARMEN	And what the fuck do you want from me?
CARCOSA	What you have always wanted. To be taken. To be held in a way which has no ending.

CARCOSA *gestures to the sister cities below.*

A GAME IN YELLOW

CARCOSA   Dread Hastur roams, and though Cassilda herself is gone, Cassilda's Scream hunts for prey along the shores of Hali below.

CASSILDA   (disembodied) Not upon us, O King, not upon us!

CARCOSA   I do not know your culture, but I shall witness it before it knows me and mine. What monsters lurk where you come from? Which city is your home?

CARMEN opens her mouth to give a hasty, automatic answer. Nothing comes out. Her brow furrows, desperate to wring the sponge of her brain for fluid knowledge.

CARMEN   New York, right?

CARCOSA   You ask me, when you should know.

CARMEN   My head hurts.

CARCOSA   Mine does not.

For the head of CARCOSA is only a pantomime of humanity. It is a thousand heads for a thousand empty spires, and the cluttered homes within that city are yellow dust at its feet. A city's soul is given by its people, and none walk that distant place now.

CARCOSA   Do you know what it is to be a ship in a bottle? A city built in miniature? Written in fiction? All the potential and brilliance, forced to be small and to suffer?

CARMEN stands resolute. Distant ululations rise, and she hears the crying of MOTHER and AJA and BLANCA and SMOKE before they fade.

    CARMEN   Is this real, or are we in the book? Am I reading you? Are you reading me?

CARCOSA descends the steps. It pities CARMEN. Here a city incarnate descends to master her, the dominant and the subservient, as she has forever craved. It is the irresistible truth of self. She may replace one influence with another. Out with the old, and long live the king.

    CARMEN   Not you. I chose Blanca.
    CARCOSA   You fled Blanca and came here. To me.

CARMEN shrinks back. An uncertainty in her face makes clear she wonders if CARCOSA is a genuine entity or a grim reflection of herself, that golden afterimage outside Rico's merely an ocular illusion and not a kingly phantom.

    CARMEN   I won't choose you, either.
    CARCOSA   You already have.

The stairs and skies fall beneath a shroud except where the two figures of CARMEN and CARCOSA stand. A vision flashes of CARMEN split open, spacious within, a stab wound in plaster with red paint for her innards.

A GAME IN YELLOW

    CARMEN   It's in me. The underside of my skin. An emptiness from head to toe, and nobody's helping me.

The shroud engulfs all the world in darkness.

    CARMEN   (disembodied) There shouldn't be a me. I don't want to *be*.

    CARCOSA   There should not be a Carmen. But there should be a Carcosa. If one fades, the other will take her place.

A thin yellow veil seizes CARMEN by the body, the face. She can no longer tell if the nothing is herself or the cloying city as the tattered fabric smothers her. She thrashes the way she play-fought BLANCA, the suffocation both monstrous and erotic, a sensuality in terror. CARMEN briefly wonders if she still sits in that apartment chair, BLANCA squeezing plastic over her face, and if everything to follow these past weeks—Underside, Smoke, The King in Yellow*—has only been an asphyxiation-driven hallucination. Dreams within blackout dreams.*

    BLANCA   (disembodied) Die for me.

CARMEN thrashes again, briefly freeing her mouth from the shroud.

    CARMEN   Where I come from—it's not like it is in here. None of this is real.

    CARCOSA   Indeed.

The all-consuming mantle of CARCOSA overtakes CARMEN, hungry for her. In this darkness, she could be everything, stretched to boundless unseen infinity. But instead, she knows her smallness. Is this shroud the garment of the King in Yellow? Has it always been, every time the stage darkened, every time CARMEN'S vision dimmed? Perhaps this shroud has loomed over CARMEN her entire life, every moment part of one erratic performance, now coming to its curtain call.

> CARMEN (struggling for breath) You think you're lonely now? You can go back to the beginning of the play and walk with everyone you've hurt all over again. Up there, it's real. If you've hurt the person you love most, and she goes, then she's gone.
>
> CARCOSA I do not dread loneliness.

CARMEN guesses this must be what being bottled feels like. Being consumed. A pure CARMEN as never was in her world, the kind that can only exist in a stage play's distilled complexity.

Perhaps this has always been her place.

> CARMEN (desperate) Because this world is you. This play. King and country. You don't understand someone walking away. And you've never had a true body, whatever isn't written in your scenes. Out there,

you need things and have to kill your body and soul to afford them. You're always a little hungry, and you're never really finished peeing. And you're full of these feelings from these out-of-control parts of your brain, and they never tell you exactly what they are or what to do with them. You just have to figure them out and hope you don't screw everything up. And it goes on like that until you die.

CARCOSA   Here, you are only real when read.

CARMEN   But I don't want to be part of the play.

The realization is the sudden chill of realizing you've forgotten to keep grieving a lost love.

CARMEN   (stern) I don't want to play anymore.

The point of her tongue jabs the back of her teeth, ready to speak a safeword into the ether. She only needs say it—dimetrodon—and stop the playing of the game.

But the yellow shroud tightens, muffling her, and only one syllable leaks out.

CARMEN   Die—

It is a doom and a curse. But CARMEN perseveres. Impossible to witness beneath the yellow-black shadows of CARCOSA, she pincers her fingers and snaps them once.

SMOKE   (disembodied) If a tree falls in the woods when no one's around, does it make a sound?

There is no sound of snapping. CARMEN tries again. She has always been capable of snapping her fingers, even as a child, when no other children could master the action. Again, again, to no end.

CASSILDA   (disembodied) Not upon us, O King, not upon us!

And here in the pain, another realization learned from CASSILDA—there is only screaming at the end of the long masquerade. And now CARMEN understands the secret.

You cannot learn this by watching a performance, and you cannot learn by reading the play. Only through the life and the dreams of the King in Yellow does clarity demonstrate to the Hyades, to the stairways and roads and waters within their black radiance, to the inhabitants of lost cities and cursed cities alike, this one simple truth:

All paths lead to dim Carcosa.

25

Unsung

CARMEN'S EYELIDS FLUTTERED OPEN, PEELING away amber skies to reveal a dim ceiling. Someone had draped one of Blanca's robes over Carmen's body, and it flowed over the side of the playroom bench where she lay, arms limp at her sides, rope marks patterning her wrists. They did not form the Yellow Sign.

Blanca appeared, expression contorted in worry. "Carmen? You there?"

"Mm." Carmen's mouth was dry. Her lips, too. A dark fog muddled her head.

"I'm sorry," Blanca said.

She spread her arms, one wrist bound in a crescent-stained ribbon of gauze, and pulled Carmen's upper body into a soft embrace. Over her shoulder, Smoke stood hugging herself.

And behind her, the stab wounds were gone from the playroom wall. Powdery red chunks littered the floor around a black shaft where Smoke had closed and abandoned her switchblade. Jagged tears parted the plaster to either side of the center, like a jacket zipper.

No writhing yellow figure looked to have emerged from within. No animals, either, great or small. There was wiring, and thin insulation, and the husks of long-dead insects.

The ordinary guts of an ordinary apartment wall.

Carmen's finger pointed. "There was nothing?"

"I think we all lost it there, momentarily," Smoke said, her tone shaky. "I meant to scare the truth out of you. Took it too far. We all said and did things we shouldn't have. I didn't have a plan of what to do. Just scared. And I'm sorry, too." She rubbed Blanca's shoulder and started to move away.

But Carmen's hand caught her wrist and pulled her into the embrace. "It's okay."

"What happened to you?" Blanca asked. She looked tearful again.

"I was stuck in a bad dream." Carmen's voice came faint, uncertain. "Now I'm awake."

Blanca and Smoke lingered until Carmen's legs felt strong enough to hold the rest of her. A fevered nervousness circled between the three of them, laced with shame. The evening would never carry on like this. Someone had to clear the air.

A sigh rattled through Carmen's lips. "We will let it go."

Smoke studied her, mouth open, maybe wanting to mention Carmen's coworkers, the play, something else, but nothing came out. Maybe she understood none of that was important now, even if she didn't know why.

A GAME IN YELLOW

"A scene we've finished playing. A game we've ended." Carmen's fingers snapped. What a curious sensation. "Dimetrodon."

It was a forgiveness, and a release. The three of them hugged again, and there was a novelty to their thrumming hearts, their uneasy breaths, miracles in their existence greater than twin suns. Greater than a play.

An echo slid through Carmen's head. *Stop reading.*

Blanca led them out of the playroom, still clutching each other, a single sorry organism of a dozen limbs clambering through the living room, turning on lights and snuffing out candles. Smoke pulled dishes from the cupboard while Blanca retrieved food from the fridge, and they sat together in chairs, unbound and yet tied together in unseen ways.

Carmen's hand guided careful bites between her lips. Eating was familiar, but the sensations came fresh. The cold of utensils against these fingertips. The light gravity of raising pierced morsels toward a face. Every movement and taste in chewing, savoring, swallowing.

On the outside, to Blanca and Smoke, this would look ordinary. They shot concerned glances at each other, worried for Carmen's welfare, but they showed no outward suspicion. Guilt shrouded their perceptiveness. They probably assumed the same of Carmen's thoughts, too absorbed in regret and self-pity to notice a difference.

On the inside, as unordinary and liminal and even strange as a plaster wall before it was torn open, yellow bricks and shining brass formed roads and foundations through Carmen's abdomen and across the underbelly of her mind. Without needless mammalian organs, there was room for hidden architecture, the building of spires where there should have been bones.

It was a different kind of masquerade, to pretend at being flesh and blood and human.

After the meal, Blanca started an animated movie and drew Smoke and what she thought was Carmen to her sides. Briefly, it noticed a city bounded by trees and flying contraptions, an artist's work come to life, but Carmen's eyes wandered. Nothing inside her head was interested in performance.

Past the couch stood the apartment windows, and what stretched beyond that glass and its vague reflections.

A city. A genuine city, not written in letters but built of hard material and perhaps harder people, each with such possibilities inside. Only in looking back on a city could you find its truth. What watched through Carmen's eyes had longed for lost places, mythical lands of captured time and music, and further back to dreamlands of flying carpets and immortal knights and snake-like emperor dragons, the stories that made up a city's soul.

It was once the same in dim Carcosa, but that soul-breaking tragedy had no name.

And it did not matter now. Here, cities stood even when their souls dripped away, leaving a hollow space where an injured spirit could rise up and fill the void, find healing respite, and then grow strong.

"Carmen?"

Blanca's questioning voice called Carmen's eyes back to her. On some scattered impulse, the city inside Carmen's flesh pressed her head forward, lips puckered, and kissed Blanca on the cheek. It then leaned past her and kissed Smoke, too.

Strange feelings spread like lightning through the body, unsettling the growing city. Her eyes fell briefly on Smoke's satchel, where that leatherbound book waited. Unimportant now.

A GAME IN YELLOW

"I need to use the restroom," Carmen's voice said.

Her body broke from the couch and moved toward the bathroom before either Blanca or Smoke could ask if she wanted them to pause the movie.

On the toilet, the body made water. After a time, it seemed to finish.

Seemed to, but nerves at the city's edges twitched with a nagging sensation of uncompletion and forgetfulness. When could it be certain this function had ended?

The city couldn't sit here forever. After making water again, it abandoned the seat and hurried to clean Carmen's paling hands.

Few ever wrote such bodily functions into plays, and certainly not for *The King in Yellow*. They simply happened offstage, assumed and unthought of by audiences and readers. But they were real—the slick faucet's stream, the soap suds forming a white cloud around the hands, the scrape of a towel across cool fingertips.

Carmen may have been right. There was more to this world than a figure from a play could guess.

Neither Blanca nor Smoke looked back when Carmen's hand opened the bathroom door. They were kissing, their minds elsewhere, their hands sliding over each other.

Carmen's lips smirked. "After all, there is a kind of bliss to it."

The city wandered into the playroom, crushing plaster fragments underfoot. Carmen's hand plucked up Smoke's switchblade and loosed the serrated steel. It gleamed a partial reflection of Carmen's face. The city then moved her toward the playroom window, where her empty hand parted the curtain and revealed a bright landscape.

This was no dim Carcosa. Beneath the black sky, every

building glowed with a hundred eyes, and the streets themselves were populous with moving forms and glowing signs of life.

Against that backdrop, a transparent reflection of Carmen's face stared back at the city behind her hazel eyes. Her pointy nose, and strong chin, and short chestnut hair.

Both cities had the option to remain as they were, the one outside the window and the one inside the flesh. The latter could abandon its intention, never filling the other's void. Never growing.

It could keep small and unimportant, relishing in the human sensations of eating food and walking through downtown. Nights of kissing and pissing and sleeping, with its own dreams to enjoy. There were movies to watch, and plays to be performed, and there was love to make, and games to play, and fucking to do, with flesh so good, it made you keep coming back, and muscles to let wither, and bones to let fuse and crack, and a mortality to make it all mean something because mortal time was brief.

Every element of life that dulled Carmen. That she took for granted.

But then, wouldn't that mean it had lured Carmen into the play solely to take her place? It remembered that, long ago, King Hastur had dragged people into the realm of the Hyades. He was a miserable, gibbering creature, long suffering from the Lake of Hali, founder of a city only in that he kept drawing pieces of other worlds to him. A soiling on the shores of Hali.

Alar was a tolerable jewel, but not the city of Hastur. There had to be better places for Carcosa than there, even past its prime.

And that was why it couldn't linger in Carmen's skin. She

A GAME IN YELLOW

was not the destination or the destiny, merely the door opened in her sleep. The possession, but only briefly. Like any life.

The city loosened the sash from the robe surrounding Carmen's body. It parted from her abdomen, exposing her soft belly. The Lake of Hali once bore fish with such white bellies, but not for the longest time. Still, the city remembered.

Carmen's fingers danced the blade downward, aiming from the underside of her fist. This would hurt, but the pain, too, would be brief.

The first stab struck to the left of Carmen's navel. The second sank into her belly on the right, forming two grim eyeholes peering from her flesh. Rich blood ran like crimson tears, one stream tracing the contours of her leg all the way to the floor, the other pooling in the coils of dark hair at her groin.

A scream writhed in Carmen's guts, and the city set Carmen's teeth against it. No interruptions, no intrusions. It was time to carve out the truth. The city had already done it to Carmen's mind, over the course of readings and dreams. Now to part the flesh.

The switchblade dragged between the belly's red eyeholes as if drawing a misplaced lipstick-clad smile. Carmen's fingers then dug underneath the makeshift flap, catching the flesh and peeling it upward. Another door to open.

There should have been organs. A rib cage.

Instead, there glowed a penetrating yellow.

Carmen's hand kept tugging, and the blade kept cutting, each doing its part to peel away the disguise that had given passage to a city undiscovered upon the maps of this world. A sense of ghostly gold reached out from the opened once-Carmen maw. A city's soul, no longer lost.

Beyond the window, concrete and steel began to quake and crumble. Their wreckage rained down on dozens at first, and then hundreds, thousands, a million screams greater than Cassilda's. They rang through the streets, echoing doom bells in Hastur as this city's hollow bloodlines filled with yellow serum. The façade of skyscrapers shattered, replaced by rising golden spires like great fingers seizing first the city and then the sky.

"Out with the old," Carmen's lips said. "And long live the king."

Carmen's pupils hovered against their whites in the glassy reflection, cast against a mounting yellow truth. One day, those pupils might form twin black suns upon the skies above Carcosa.

All it needed to do was cut them away. Free them to become one with the heavens.

Carmen's hands lifted the switchblade to her face. Steel teeth aimed for the white flesh of an eyeball, and then a cheek, a jawline. Places for fingers to grasp and tug.

New screams cut through the air from behind Carmen's head. Perhaps they were Blanca and Smoke. Perhaps they were a dream.

"Carmen, what are you doing?"

"Is that blood?"

"No, no, no, no!"

"Don't let her—"

But the shouts were dying, and the city couldn't pay attention to them now. It was leaving this spot, its roots spreading into the lights beyond the window.

A GAME IN YELLOW

The peeling of flesh gave way to a brief grin in the glass reflection before the last of the disguise tore away, same as the city.

Another voice—not Carmen's—thundered from between her teeth.

"No. Mask."

ACKNOWLEDGMENTS

When a writer talks about how long it takes to write a book, it's often about the typing, the span of time from starting that first chapter to ending the last, along with revisions, rereads, and so on.

But that measurement of time leaves out how long the story haunted them first. Some of these story ghosts are easier to catch than others, and the difficult ones bother us for a long, long time, unwilling to leave and yet as useless as hauntings tend to be until finally they either move on or, in my case, possess me until I exorcise them through writing.

That was the case here. The plot didn't haunt so much as the characters. Carmen, Blanca, and Smoke haunted me for some time. I'd written interactions between them, knew their personalities, but it took a while for me to understand what they were doing here and why they wouldn't leave me alone.

Eventually, I took on some of Carmen's obsessive nature and became a bit obsessed with them myself. And when their story at last took shape and possessed me, I took to exorcising all of them with a feverish passion.

That exorcism is this book, the telling of these three women crashing into each other and the old horror that looms over them. Maybe that's one reason to write horror. When characters

ACKNOWLEDGMENTS

haunt you enough that you have to write their story, sometimes you write about haunting them right back. You could call it narrative vengeance. Or flirting with disaster, depending on how disastrous the characters can be.

To balance out a little of Carmen's disastrousness, I'll say that any interest in kink should involve research. Real research, not rumors or fictional depictions, regardless of their medium. Any practice should involve the consent and safety of all participants. There are a hundred reasons to get into kink, such as sexual gratification, closeness with partners, exploring different facets of intimacy, a better understanding for respect and boundaries, spiritual transcendence—the list goes on, often blending together. But for real, and I cannot emphasize this enough, *safety first*.

Cursed books, on the other hand? No research needed; just go wild. Life is short.

This book, cursed or not, could never have existed without the brilliant foundational text of Robert W. Chambers. Though he did not invent Carcosa—that credit belongs to Ambrose Bierce with his short story "An Inhabitant of Carcosa," who instilled it with a lost and haunted atmosphere—Chambers did create our popular understanding of it, and much of the mythology surrounding it, along with the cursed play *The King in Yellow* and its original stories that have spawned thousands of retellings, explorations, and deviations in the past 130 years. Thank you for the long-lived nightmares.

More immediate thanks go to my agent, Lane Heymont, who might be some kind of magician with the encouraging miracles he pulls off.

ACKNOWLEDGMENTS

My sincerest gratitude to Joe Monti, Caroline Tew, Crystal Watanabe, Yvette Grant, and the entire Saga team. I'm exceptionally lucky to be working with these brilliant people. Also my thanks go to Math Monahan and Caroline Teagle for their amazing art design and evocative cover art.

A thank-you also to the readers and booksellers who make all this possible.

There are too many friends to mention here who I lean on frequently, whether they're aware of it or not, whether from their profound insights or from giving me a moment's brightness on grim days. Sara, Jess, Gabino, Rachel, Becky, Brian, Laurel, you are all so wonderful. Thank you, Cina, for ceaselessly bopping me with a reassurance mallet through this whole thing. And Suzan, you've championed me again and again when I'm facing my greatest foe—myself—and I think you know who's going to win. I'm forever grateful. This is one of those books, like *Queen of Teeth*, that I don't think my heart would've been in the right place to write if not for Claire Holland being part of my life and inspiring me to be my whole vivacious self.

And as always, thanks to my darling J, who will never read this book, but encouraged every moment of my writing it with love and zeal.